The Treasures
of
Boo-Ditch

To Sandy's grandchildren. Have fun reading. Sonja Olsen

By
SONJA OLSEN

Illustrated by
The Students of St. Francis Xavier Catholic School
Brunswick, Georgia

Printed by
CreateSpace.com

Olsen, Sonja, 1933-
The Treasures of Boo-Ditch/by Sonja Olsen - 1ˢᵗ ed.

Summary: Two young girls, one physically normal and one who is physically
disabled, share adventures in a remote part of an island in Georgia where they
create their own entertainment coping with disabilities and forming a bond that
lasts a lifetime.

ISBN: 146095372X
ISBN 13: 9781460953723

Dedicated to my grandson,
William Wallace Kimmell

Acknowledgments

I want to thank Jerry Edwards, a member of the third family that lived on Gascoigne Bluff, St. Simons Island, Ga. during the 30's and 40's for making it possible for me to publish this book; Jacqui Willey, whom I knew in Atlanta who gave me the idea of telling the story to my grandson;and Mardith Johnston for suggesting having students in the art clubs at St. Francis Xavier Catholic School illustrate the book.

The illustrations are the works of the students in the three after-school art clubs at St. Francis instructed by Mardith and Debbie Doliveria, St. Francis' art teacher. A special heart-felt thanks to Mardith and Debbie and to all the students who participated in this endeavor.

Last but not least, my mother, Lillie Mae Olsen, who gave me the freedom to wander and use my imagination and my father, Olaf H. Olsen who was my childhood encourager.

Illustrations and Illustrators

Chapter 2
The Hide-a-ways: Jonathan Carden, 8th Grade;
Marco Passinite, 4th Grade

Chapter 3
The Frederica Bridge: Gabrielle Azumbuja;
The Tug Boat: Kelsey Ann Cabiness, 3rd Grade

Chapter 4
Walking to the Dock: Maggie Hummel, 3rd Grade

Chapter 5
The Map: The Author

Chapter 6
The Burning Teepee: Greta Carter, 4th Grade

Chapter 8
The Fiddlers: Jonathan Carden, 8th Grade; Ladd Rector,
5th Grade; Dylan McHugh, 3rd Grade; Kia Patel, 2nd Grade;
Kyle Strasser, 3rd Grade,
Rescuing the Box: Mason McGraw, 3rd Grade

Chapter 9
Shelling the Road: Sally Brock, 3rd Grade

Chapter 11
The Tree with the Nail and Stob: Will Brown, 7th Grade

Contents

(1)

Will and His Grandma

After a period of silence, interrupted only with "uh huhs," Will said, "Goodbye."

"That your mom?" I asked.

"You bet," Will said

"Final Instructions?"

"Yeah! As usual. Don't watch TV. Brush your teeth. Help your grandma."

"Well, that's not so bad, except for the TV. We may have to find a good movie on the TV. A good spy movie, maybe?"

It was semester break. Will, my ten-year-old grandson was spending a few days with me. His parents were taking his sister back to college and he didn't want to go. I was glad for him to stay. We were buddies and had planned some daily side trips around Atlanta.

The phone rang again! Will picked up the receiver. "Hello" he grunted. Then his tone changed. "This is Will. I'm Sonja's grandson."

"Sonja, it's for you," Will said handing me the phone. For some reason ever since he was about three years old, Will has called me by my given name and not 'Maw Maw', my grandma name. "Do you know someone named Charlie Carr?."

"Sure, He's the nephew of my childhood playmate, Woodie. She had a sister who was 14 years older. I haven't seen or heard from him in years."

Wondering what this was about, I took the phone., "Hello, Charlie," I said.

The voice at the other end was solemn. "Sonja, I just wanted you to know that Woodie passed away yesterday."

"My goodness, Charlie, I just visited her recently. She looked a lot older, but her spirits were good. What happened?"

"In the last few weeks her health has been declining. She was so fragile. She couldn't make it," Charlie explained.

Woodie, although thin and fragile looking had really been strong. I was surprised to hear the terrible news.

"We're having a grave side service at 4 o'clock tomorrow. Only the family will be present, but we would like for you to be there." Charlie said.

"Thanks, Charlie, I appreciate your considering me one of the family. Woodie and I were the best of friends and I am so sorry to hear this sad news. Where will the service be?"

"It will be at Christ Church Cemetery on the Island."

"I'll be there--and my grandson will be with me, if that's Okay?" Will had never been to St. Simons. This change of plans shouldn't disappoint him. Only the opposite--he should be very excited.

"Sure, that's fine." Charlie said.

"Thank you for calling, Charlie. Good bye."

As I absent-mindedly placed the telephone in its cradle, my mind drifted back to the last time I had seen Woodie.

Of course I'd be there--Woodie was my best friend, with whom I had shared a creative childhood. I had helped her through all the physical challenges she faced, and Woodie had taught me patience and adaptability.

Our last visit had only been three weeks earlier. Woodie lived alone, cherishing her independence despite the serious handicap. Both parents had lived well into their nineties, her mother passing away only two years ago. Her sister had died of cancer many years ago.

When Woodie's father retired from the Sea Island Nursery, the family had to move out of the company home and bought property on Frederica Road. There they built the house where she still lived.

While parking in the driveway, I noticed a note tacked to the back door. At the door: It read, "OCCUPANT IN WHEEL CHAIR. IT WILL TAKE TIME TO ANSWER. DON'T GO AWAY." I was surprised. Woodie suffered damage to her motor nerves at birth. We called her a "spastic." As an adult she told me she had Cerebral Palsy, but she had never used a wheel- chair. She treasured the self-reliance which she struggled so hard for as a child.

Her knees were twisted in, and she always walked jerking one foot in front of the other. Her arms flailed as if in a spasm and her head leaned to one side. Slurred words came from her drooling mouth, but she had never been an invalid. She was too determined to do what able children did.

That day I rang the bell and waited but no one came to the door; I heard no sounds. I peeked into the back door window but saw nothing, and thought she might be sleeping so I rang the bell several more times. Assuming she wasn't at home, I turned to walk down the steps. At that moment, a black car pulled into the driveway, driven by an older woman. When she got out of the car, I introduced myself and asked if Woodie were home and if I might see her.

"She's home, but I'll have to ask her," she replied, unlocking the back door. I assumed she must be a housekeeper.

"What's your name?" she asked briskly, closing the screen door.

"Sonja", I repeated as she slammed the back door leaving me standing on the steps.

Dismayed at being questioned about seeing Woodie, I began to wonder what condition she might be in. Only once had I been left standing outside Woodie's door. That was the time

I left Woodie playing alone in the yard to race up the shell road on my bike with one of the boys who lived in back of us who had stopped to chat. Woodie's mother came home, and seeing I had left Woodie alone, became angry and taken her home.

The race finished, I rode back home. Not seeing Woodie in the yard, I pedaled to her house. I didn't even have time to get off my bike before her mother was outside to give me a tongue lashing for leaving Woodie alone.

Embarrassed and hurt, I went home, and never told anyone.

My memories were interrupted when the housekeeper opened the back door. She curtly said, "Woodie, will see you. I'll show you where her room is." I opened the screen door and walked into the kitchen.

I was led through unlit rooms to her bright and cheery bedroom, where Woodie sat on the side of her bed. Several glasses half full of what looked like water were on a tray beside the bed. As usual, her head was leaning to one side, but now she had on a neck collar. Her hair was gray and hadn't been combed. I hugged her and sat in the wheelchair beside her bed. Her thin pink nylon gown hung off one boney shoulder. When greeting me she was smiling and seemed in good spirits, but looked old. We were the same age, but I thought she could be ten years older.

"Woodie, don't you know it's time to get out of bed? It's past noon." I said and leaned down to give her a hug.

"Yeah, I know. What are you doing here?" she asked to change the subject.

"Looking for a place to live. I've decided to move back home soon."

"Are you retiring?" She asked.

"Don't you think I'm old enough? You know how old I am! "I jested.

"Remember, Boo-Ditch?" she said changing the subject and bringing back memories of our childhood.

"I'll never forget it." I responded.

"Those were fun days. Sonja, you were my best friend. You treated me like I was normal," she said.

"Why shouldn't I have treated you like that? You were pretty tough." I said. "Besides, we only had each other. No one else our age lived near us."

"You're still my best friend," I added with warmth. "I'm sorry I didn't keep in touch as I should have. After college I moved away, married, worked outside the home and raised two children."

"Well, we each took on new responsibilities" she replied. "I worked at the Pulp Mill and helped Mom and Dad in their flower shop. I was busy, too."

The suffocating heat in the room shortened my stay. After we had laughed about the things we did as children, I got up to leave and gave her a big bear hug.

"When I move here, we can get together," I said

"Sounds good to me!" she said.

"You get out of bed so we can explore again and maybe we can find Boo-ditch and our buried treasure," I said from the doorway.

That was the last time I saw her.

"What's wrong, Sonja?" Will queried, jolting me back to reality.

"Woodie died. Her funeral is tomorrow on St. Simons" I told him. "Would you be disappointed if we changed our plans and went to the island?

"The island? The Island? Take me to the island? Gee, that sounds awesome. Are you kidding? But, who's Woodie?"

"Do you really want to know?"

"Sure— or I wouldn't have asked."

The need to share the story of days Woodie and I spent together as children surfaced. "Do you want to know enough to turn off the television and listen to a long story?"

Will grabbed the remote control and dramatically pushed the "off" button. We settled on the sofa together and I began recalling my childhood of over sixty years ago.

(2)

Hide-a-Ways

"Woodie and I had many hide-a-ways where we spent long hours playing. Our summer hide-a-way was under one end of her back porch which stood five feet off the ground. A large eleagnus bush, its dull green leaves with tiny rust colored spots, covered the entrance and provided welcome shade on hot humid days. It was always cool under the porch.

On rainy days we took shelter under the porch, too, and made mud pies. Coffee cans caught plenty of rain water, and the black dirt floor provided lots of dough. We called this hide-a-way, "Mud Pie Kitchen."

Another hide-a-way was in my front yard with mother's wooden Adirondack lawn chairs. We made the hide-a-way by turning four chairs down with the backs forming the roof. They were arranged in a square making the entire inside enclosed.

Each chair seat and its arms formed a cubbyhole giving us four cubbyholes. To become entirely invisible, we draped the top and sides with Spanish moss that had fallen to the ground. Under canopies of moss hanging between the slats we could sit for hours hidden from the world: reading, making up stories and plotting our next adventure. We called this hide-a-way, "Mossy Chairs."

But our favorite hide-a-way was in the middle of a large stand of bamboo that flourished behind Woodie's house surrounded by a patch of scrubby oaks covered with thorny vines. With the help of mother's hedge clippers, we cleared a path to our inner sanctum.

It was like walking into a huge cathedral, where the silence was only broken by a breeze gently rustling the long narrow leaves of the willowy branches growing from the polished green bamboo canes. The light through the lush growth feebly flickered as through a stained glass window. The fully shaded ground was covered with a toast-colored carpet of slender dead leaves woven in a zig-zag pattern. It was the perfect hide-a-way.

Two Renditions of the Three Hide-a-Ways

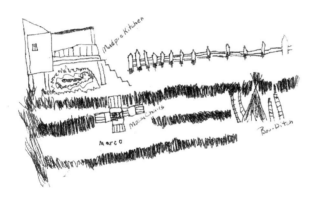

Woodie's father was manager of the nursery located next to her house. With his chief gardener, King, he built us a teepee in this stand of bamboo pulling together several canes of bamboo and tying them together at the top with twine. This cone-shaped frame, high enough for us to stand up inside, was draped with brown-coarse-woven "croaker" sacks attached with long wires threaded through the fabric and twisted around a bamboo pole. One piece of cloth near the bottom hung loose forming the entrance to our dwelling.

Next to the teepee in our bamboo forest was a ditch—actually just a long shallow depression in the earth. It wasn't wide or deep and we could jump across it. However, we built a bamboo bridge anyway. A lone oak pushing out of the ground at the other end of the bridge had probably grown from an acorn buried by a squirrel.

We named this hide-a-way ***Boo-Ditch***."

I glanced at the living room clock.

"That's all for tonight, Will. We have to leave early in the morning to be there by 3 o'clock.

"Ahh, Sonja."

"No, 'Ahh, Sonja.' It's bedtime. Besides you have at least four hours to hear the rest of the story as we are driving."

"Okay. Good night, Sonja," Will surrendered as he gave me a big goodnight hug.

(3)

Getting on the Island

We were well on our way to Macon, cruising along I-75, before Will smiled and reminded me of my promise.

"Sonja, have your forgotten? You said you'd finish your story. I'm ready!"

"Me, too," I assured him. "We can start by crossing some wooden bridges."

"Gosh, wooden bridges?" Will exclaimed. "Are they covered? Can only one car cross them at a time?"

"No, the bridges aren't covered, "I chuckled, "and the way my mom drove you'd think they could only carry one car at a time."

The island where Woodie and I live is joined to the mainland by a black tar ribbon causeway weaving through the green marshlands and studded with five rickety wooden bridges.

As our car bumped across the first bridge, its clattering planks frighten the fiddler crabs sunning along the edge of the road sending them scurrying into their holes.

On that day I was less interested in fiddler crabs than in listening to the rattling of the planks. 'Kerplunk, kerplunk, kerplunk.' Mother drove slowly across all five bridges, but slowest across this one because she had to stop and pay toll at the end of this bridge.

Driving up to the toll house mother said, "Sonja, look in my change purse and get out a dime. Would you give it to Mr. Evans?"

Mr. Evans was the tollman.

"Sure" I said opening the small change purse. I was sitting in the back seat and rolled down the window on the driver's side.

"Hello, miss," Mr. Evans said as I handed him the money.

"Hi, Mr. Evans."

He handed me the ticket receipt. "Take good care of your mom."

As mother shifted back into first gear, I said, "Sure will, Mr. Evans." All the toll keepers knew me.

Mother had been shopping downtown and had come by my school to pick me up, as she often did when she was on the mainland. I was glad she had come today. It was Friday and Woodie and I had things to plan for Saturday. Woodie was already home. Because of her handicap she went to a small private school on Sea Island, which only had five students. Since there were no public schools on the St. Simons, I went to the mainland to school.

"Sonja, how much homework do you have?" mother asked as we approached the second bridge.

"Not any." I replied. "It's Friday. We don't have homework on Fridays."

A car was coming across the bridge towards us. Even though there were two lanes, mother put on the brakes and waited until the other car has passed before continuing across.

"Mom, you had plenty of room. Why stop? We'll never get home." I said.

"What's your big hurry, Miss Priss?" mother said while her eyes were glued to the bridge. "You're getting home earlier than if you had taken the bus,"

She slowed down again on the approach to the other end of the bridge, and again over two more bridges.

Mother only expected the worst from these rickety bridges. For one thing, cars driving over the planks might make nails pop up and loosen the planks. When it rained the planks were very slippery and a skid could send us through the wooden railing into the river. But stopping and waiting for a car to pass—that seemed extreme.

Mother was a small lady with a strong will. She had a lot of spunk and could be sassy at times. She guarded her children, but not to the point of being possessive. She wanted to protect us from dangers, but she still showed confidence in each of us. It was hard for me to understand that she let Woodie and me roam the woods with snakes and bugs and all types of hazards, but was so careful going off and on bridges. She even let me fish by myself on the docks and play at the river. I could have fallen into the water or been kidnaped by some stranger.

At the last bridge, I rolled down the window with the toll ticket in my other hand ready to give Mr. Chitty, the toll house keeper on the island.

Traffic was slow and the sun was shining. Mr. Chitty was probably rocking in rhythm to the river in the big rocking chair on the porch of the small white clapboard tollhouse.

The last bridge was a drawbridge. Anytime a boat came down the river, the cars were stopped on the bridge and the draw span opened so it could continue down the river.

Three long blasts from a boat on the river ahead caused my heart to sink.

"Mom, don't stop. Let's get across the bridge, "I urged."

"Can't," mother said creeping along. "Mr. Chitty has already closed the gates to traffic coming off the island. I have to stop"

I looked ahead. Mr. Chitty was indeed ambling toward the gate in front of our car.

Down the river a tug boat with two barges in tow was heading our way. Its three horn blasts had signaled Mr. Chitty to open the drawbridge and let it pass through.

"Hey, Mr. Chitty," I said jumping onto the bridge waving my hands. "I'll close these gates for you." Mr. Chitty waved a "thank you" and turned back to the middle of the draw span.

"Be careful, Sonja," Mother continued.

"I was just being helpful. Mr. Chitty doesn't hurry for anything."

After closing the gates I stood beside our car to watch the bridge-opening ceremony. Mr. Chitty looked like an ant beneath the towering criss-crossed steel beams of the draw span. Leaning over the side, he pulled up a big slanted upside down "L"-shaped pipe with a round metal collar at the bottom.

Helping Mr. Chitty

"Mom, that must be heavy. Look how Mr. Chitty struggles to lift it into the lock." I said. Mother had gotten out of the car too, mainly to hold onto me. She must have thought I would fall off the bridge.

"Yes, it is heavy." mother agreed.

We stood there together engrossed in the same scene we'd witnessed so many times. The funny shaped device used to unlock the drawspan was now in place. Mr. Chitty kept pushing the extended handle as he walked in wide circles to unlock the draw span. Slowly the span began to turn.

Today it was taking longer than usual. "Gee, Mom," I said "We'll be here an hour. That tug boat is way up the river."

"Would you rather have the bridge knocked down?" Mother barbed.

"Uh oh," I thought. "Mom's getting peeved with me. I'd better keep quiet." I turned to look at the tug boat. It was pulling two enormous barges that lay low in the water.

"The tug with its barges can't circle in the middle of the river waiting on the bridge to open." Mother continued noting my silence. "The captain has to get Mr. Chitty out on that bridge and the span opened before the tug even gets near. I guess the captain knows Mr. Chitty never hurries. You want to take a boat ride to school every morning? That's the only way to get off this island if that tug rams this rickety bridge."

"Gee, Mom, that's not a bad idea. Dad could take us in his boat everyday." I joked.

"You do like adventure." Mother quipped.

"Well, the Captain got Mr. Chitty out in plenty of time today." I said looking at him as he leaned on the railing of the opened span watching the tug slowly advance. As the tug with its half-sunken barges chugged past, I became curious.

"Mom, what do you think the barges are carrying?" I asked. "I don't see anything on top of them."

"It's probably oil or gasoline inside the barge. That's why the barges are so low in the water" she said. "They travel the inland waterway through the rivers along the coast of the United States. This river is part of that inland waterway."

I knew that. If you went "outside" you were traveling in the ocean. If you went "inside" you traveled the rivers. I'd lived on this river all my ten years, seeing yachts and tugs and barges and even Ripley's Chinese JUNK go past.

Hadn't I run to the dock in front of the house when I heard the horn blasts? Other times I had looked out the upstairs windows. Sometimes at night the search light from the boats looking for the shore lines shone into our windows like a one eyed-monster.

The tug with its barges had finally chugged past. Mr. Chitty had locked the bridge and was putting up the "opener."

"Sonja, open the gates at this end. Then Mr. Chitty won't have to walk so much." Mother suggested as she got into the car.

I signaled to Mr. Chitty. He saw me and headed toward the island to unlock the gates for the cars coming toward the mainland.

As we came off the bridge onto the island, I handed Mr. Chitty the toll ticket. "You're a mighty good helper," he said patting my hand.

Mother turned immediately to the left down the oyster shell road that led to my house and Woodie's.

(4)

Planning for Saturday

Mom drove the car into our yard. Woodie was sitting in the rocking chair on the front porch. My dog, Punky, was sleeping on the steps.

I opened the car door and jumped out before mother turned off the engine. Punky jumped up, wagging his tail.

"Not so fast, young lady," Mother said. "Change your clothes before you go to play."

"Okay," I said, petting Punky on the head. "Down! Down! Good dog!"

Grabbing Woodie by both hands, I pulled her up out of the chair. She had been waiting for me to do that. "Oops! Almost pulled too hard," I said as I put one foot in back to brace myself.

"Let's go upstairs. I'll change and we can go somewhere out of the earshot of my brother and sisters to plot something."

"Let's go to the Boat Club. No one will hear us there," Woodie said with her familiar slur. Many people didn't understand her, but I did; so I became her interpreter on many occasions.

"Only the birds, squirrels and Punky. But he'll be busy chasing the fiddlers," she added.

"Where are you two going in such a big hurry?" my older sister, Brigit–whom we called Bee Bee—cross examined us.

"None of your business," I hurled back before Woodie had a chance to answer. Woodie waited as I changed into my overalls, then we headed quickly down the stairs. "Mom," I yelled as we went out the door, "we'll be at the Boat Club!"

We slowed down at the far side of the yard, silently watching chalky dust billow from under our feet as we kicked shells crushed to pieces by the cars driving over them.

On the way to the dock to plan for Saturday

Standing on the bluff we could see the deserted dock where once the wealthy stored their boats.

"I wonder what happened," Woodie said. "The dock is still there, but the boathouse is gone. There's nothing left, but a big U-shaped dock and a big open space where the boat house was."

"I don't know, but whatever, it's a great place to play."

"Hey! Come on! Let's slide down the bluff!" Woodie said.

Grabbing Woodie's hand, I started running and pulling her. This was our game. By holding her hand, I provided support to keep her from falling, and when I pulled her, the sensation of going so fast made her stomach tickle; a feeling she always loved.

"Wheeee" we screamed. holding hands before sliding down the bluff on our feet to Punky as he waited for us at the bottom.

Like always, we tumbled over at the bottom and rolled a couple of feet. We weren't hurt, but very sandy.

We brushed off our clothes and walked onto the dock as Punky ran off to go exploring. Between the planks on the dock we watched fiddler crabs scampering into their burrows in the mud.

A cool gentle breeze blew from the northeast down the river causing a chill from the sweat running down our cheeks.

"I'm cold," said Woodie shivering.

In the middle of the abandoned dock was an empty wooden storage bin large enough for us both to fit inside. "That's the perfect place," Woodie said pointing to the bin. "It will keep the wind off.

"We'd better get this meeting started. The sun is low in the sky and once it starts sinking, it sinks fast," I said.

A 4" x 4" block of wood on the dock became a step for the bin. Woodie stepped up on the block, and with my holding her, she lifted her legs over one at a time to the inside of the bin. I scrambled in after her. We sat facing each other, our back against opposite ends of the bin and legs stretched out to each other's side.

We huddled together like conspirators.

"Okay, you first," I told her. "What are our great plans for tomorrow?"

"Okay," Woodie said, her eyes alight. "Since Boo-ditch is ours, why don't we lay claim to it?"

"Sure," I agreed. "But how do we do that?"

"We bury a treasure there," she said.

"Great, like pirates. But what do we have to bury?" I asked.

"Well, how about our most prized possessions?" she suggested.

"But I don't want to bury my favorite things in the dirt," I said.

"Can't you do without it for a year? Then we'll dig it up."

I could tell she'd spent a lot of time thinking about this. Probably while I'd been out fishing by myself.

"Okay, let me think then. I'll have to look in my junk box."

"Me too," Woodie said thoughtfully.

"Let's also bring a secret treasure. Something we really treasure," I added.

"But it won't be a secret if you see it when we fill the treasure chest," she responded.

"I was thinking of something we might like to share with each other, but not right now-only when we dig up the treasure will we know what the other has put in the chest."

With a puzzling look Woodie agreed, then asked, "Do you have a treasure chest?"

"No, but I have a tin box cookies came in last Christmas. It kind of looks like a treasure chest," I added

"We'll have to figure a way to keep water out," she said.

After debating for a while about the best way to keep the treasures safe, we settled on covering the tin with wax. There were some candles and matches in the teepee, and we agreed to bring more.

But we never discussed what treasures we were going to bring.

The big orange-red ball slid behind the trees on the mainland as we hurriedly finished our plans for the next day.

I climbed out first reaching back to put the block of wood inside the bin for Woodie to step on. Then I grabbed her under her arms as she lifted each leg out over the edge of the bin. She rolled out sideways while I kept her from falling on the dock.

"Here, Punky! Let's go," I called.

Punky came running with mud on his paws, and led the way up the bluff. I grabbed Woodie's hand to pull her up the sandy bluff. I was tired when we got to the top fighting the sand and the weight of Woodie. Back at the road we turned to see a pale-blue sky streaked with pink clouds, quickly turning grey as evening fell around us.

"See you at 8 o'clock tomorrow morning," Woodie said hobbling on the road to her house with Punky for company.

The shades of darkness drew slowly across the sky, and the lights inside my house glowed with warmth. I could hear my sister, Cecilia, practicing the piano.

Opening the front door I was greeted by the strong odor of fish frying.

"Gosh, mom. Is that the fish I caught yesterday? I asked with pride.

"Sure is" she answered, "and we have grits to go along with them.

"Mmmmmm," I said. Grits and butter and fried fresh fish; there was nothing better. Especially since I had caught the fish.

"Well, go upstairs and wash your hands. Tell your big sister and brother to get ready, too." Mother instructed. "I'll get the concert pianist."

As I jaunted up the steps, I smelled tobacco smoke coming from my brother's room and stuck my head in. He was smoking a pipe. "Mom says to get ready for supper," I said. "Hey, let me have a puff."

"Okay! Here!" he said stretching out the pipe to me as I walked into the room.

I held the bowl of the pipe with my fingers, put the stem between my lips and took a puff. "Ugh" I said spitting on the floor.

"That's nasty. How can you stand it? It bit my tongue," I said as I ran to the bathroom and grabbed my tooth brush to brush the taste off my tongue.

He laughed. "Serves you right. You're too young to smoke."

"Yeah, Yeah! Then why did you let me?" I asked.

"To teach you a lesson," he retorted.

'I'll teach him a lesson,' I thought. 'He's always pestering me.' I had seen his pocket knife lying on the table beside his bed. I planned to use it on Saturday plus a few other choice items in his room.

Coming out of the bathroom into the bedroom shared by us three girls, Bee Bee lying on the bed studying raised her nose out of the book and asked, "What was that about?"

"Oh, just giving my teeth a good cleaning before supper. Mom said to wash up and come on down, supper is almost ready." I said.

"By the way, Sonja, what are you and Woodie going to do tomorrow? I am sure you have something special planned." my big sister asked sarcastically.

"Oh, we're going to Boo-Ditch. Maybe we'll find a pirate lurking among the bamboo canes burying a treasure." I said.

"I don't believe a word you say. You never tell the truth," she said while getting off the bed. "But you do make a good storyteller."

"Supper's ready. Come on down," mother called from the bottom of the stairs.

Our kitchen was long and narrow. The stove, sink and cupboards formed a "U" at one end. At the other end was the table where we ate. We entered by the table and if we kept on going straight would walk out the back door. The refrigerator was against the wall next to the back door.

The three of us sprang down the stairs and scrambled to our seats. "Where's the prima donna?" my brother asked. We all laughed. All, except Mother. "That's no way to talk about your sister. She works hard." she scolded. Just then the "prima donna" walked in.

"Sonja, you say the Blessing." Mother instructed. We all folded our hands while I whizzed through the Norwegian blessing.

I had no sooner said, "Amen" when the front door opened and in walked Daddy. "Never fails," Mom said. "The minute we sit down to eat, your dad comes home."

As Daddy kissed her on the cheek, she told him "Good timing."

"Got a late start from Cumberland Island. I decided to dock in front of the house. Kept you from having to come across the causeway at night to the boatyard to pick me up."

"Thanks," Mom said gratefully.

"It would be midnight before she got there, the way she creeps across those bridges," I wisecracked. We had only one car.

No one laughed. Dad clicked his fingers and pointed upstairs. I'd said the wrong thing at the wrong time. I took my grits and fish upstairs and ate by myself. I was sorry I had said that, but now my thoughts as I ate alone were on what special treasure would I take tomorrow.

(5)

Boo-Ditch

The next morning I awakened early. The aroma of fresh coffee drifting up to my room induced me to jump out of bed instantly. I knew dad was up. I hurried down the stairs, gave dad a hug and a kiss on the cheek.

"Want to ride with me on the boat?" Dad asked."I have to take it back to the boatyard in Brunswick.

"Gosh, Dad, I wish I had known that yesterday," I said as I took a cup and filled it half with coffee and half with milk. "Woodie and I have made great plans for today. I'd rather be on the boat with you," I said regretfully, thinking how I couldn't disappoint Woodie. She was my best friend, but sometimes I wished she was normal. Dad would have taken her, too if she wasn't....crippled! There! I said the word to myself. Crippled!

I gave him a hug. He understood how I felt. "Sonja, it takes a lot of courage to stick by someone, but also you had better quit wisecracking on your mother's driving on the bridges."

"Oh, Dad, you could have gone all day without saying that. I knew the minute those words slipped out last night that I shouldn't have said them. She had just taken so long to drive home yesterday."

"I know, but she is a safe driver. She doesn't want you to get hurt." Opening the screen door, Dad turned around and blew a kiss. "See you this afternoon. You and Woodie have a great adventure."

I turned and went upstairs to my brother's room. His face was buried in the pillow. He was still in deep sleep. He didn't move as I tiptoed around his room taking from his desk what I needed for the day.

I peeked into the bedroom where us three girls slept. My sisters were still asleep, too.

Mother got out of bed while I was in the bathroom dressing. She was in the kitchen drinking her cup of "creamed" coffee, eating toast topped with orange marmalade, and listening to the local news on the radio.

I didn't want her to question me about what was in the metal box I was carrying, so I by-passed the kitchen door and went out the front door.

"I'm going to Woodie's," I called back into the house.

As I opened the front door Punky was noisily scrambling into the house, so I couldn't hear what mother said. But I knew it was 'Be careful. Watch out for snakes.'

Snakes! Snakes! This was wintertime. No snakes slithered around in the woods when it was cold. Snakes seemed to be her only concern.

I walked toward Woodie's under the massive old live oak trees, which had been lining our road for hundreds of years. They were beautiful and filled with mystery for two little girls with vivid imaginations.

One especially bewitching oak towered over a curve in the road between our houses. Its graceful branches bent down to within a few feet of the ground so Woodie and I could pull it down as the first step into its limbs' myriad twists and turns. It gave us a comfortable perch from which we might settle back and look out through its many leaves across what seemed to be miles of "our land."

We promised to meet halfway between our houses along this grand avenue, near our special oak tree. I was there. Woodie was nowhere in sight. She always came early. What had happened?

Had her mother told her to stay home? I didn't think so; she was always glad for Woodie to go outside and play.

Just in case she was near I called out, "Woodie! Woodie!" There was no answer, but I heard what I thought was a giggle.

"Okay, Woodie, where are you hiding?" I yelled. "That was you giggling!"

Suddenly I heard a crash and looked around to find Woodie lying on the ground under the big tree.

"How in the world did you climb up that limb?" I squealed, grabbing her hand to help her stand. But she jerked her hand away.

"Let go of me. I climbed that limb and I can get myself up," she told me emphatically.

"Okay, Okay, get up by yourself, I just hope you're not hurt."

"No I'm not," she reassured me.

"Great, then let's get on with our treasure burying." I said. "That sack you brought looks pretty heavy. What'cha got in it anyway?"

Avoiding my question she said, "I don't see Punky following you."

"He ran into the house when I opened the door. He's such a pest. Always trying to get into our teepee," I said before repeating "Woodie, what's in your sack? Everything isn't a secret."

"Let's wait until we get to Boo-Ditch," Woodie dismissed my curiosity for the third time. "I brought a red bandana to wrap all of the treasures in. Did you get the knife?"

"Yeah, my brother was still sleeping so I got his pocket knife off his desk and two boxes of stick matches that were beside his pipe. Hope he doesn't miss them. The shovel is already in the teepee."

So we turned in the direction of her house and were soon cutting across her back yard. When we entered the overgrown bamboo grove, silence closed in around us. Our dark "secret" alcove was flickering again with rays of winter light sifting through the flimsy branches.

Red ribbons tied on some of the canes guided us to our hideout, and blue ribbons were there to show the way in from the other direction–Woodie's father insisted we have a marked path so we wouldn't get lost. Soon we arrived at the small clearing and our teepee.

"Check out the teepee, Woodie, for varmints" I ordered. "I'll look outside around the teepee to see if there are any snakes."

There really were varmints back then...raccoons, 'possoms. Snakes! Oh, we had seen our share. Once Woodie I were walking down the road with her mother, nephew and niece when her nephew jumped over what he thought was a bundle of Spanish moss. Then the "bundle of moss" moved. It was a rattlesnake! Woodie's mother grabbed a big stick and pounded it to a pulp.

"Coast is clear," Woodie said sticking her head out the opening. "Only your shovel, the coffee can with candles and matches."

"Okay outside, too," I said crawling inside.

We settled ourselves Indian style on the ground. Taking a candle, I struck a match, heated the bottom of the candle and stuck it on the top of the "upside down" empty coffee can. Then I lit the candle.

In the soft candle light, we started revealing our treasures before placing them on the bandana spread out between us on the ground.

"Gee, Woodie. Where did you get that diamond brooch?" I asked

"Those are rhinestones, not diamonds," she corrected me. "And the catch is broken. Anyway, it's none of your business where I got it." she sassily retorted.

"Well. Okay! Okay!" I said, insulted by her rebuff.

Woodie pulled a fountain pen from her bag, a Schaeffer without any ink. Then with a flourish she dropped onto the red cloth a string of blue glass beads and a corsage pin onto a corner of the red cloth.

"What do you have?" she asked.

"Well, here's a buffalo nickel and a greenish aggie." I said.

"Looks like a marble to me. Where'd you get it?" Woodie asked.

"It is a marble. It's a shooter." I answered. "It's made of agate, so 'aggie' is what they're called. And it's none of your business where I got it. Turn about's fair play." Actually my brother had given it to me to keep quiet when I spied on him sticking arrows down in the graves in the old cemetery in the woods behind our house.

"All right! What else do you have? Woodie asked.

"Two bobbie pins and a tiny copy of the Gospel of John," I said putting the little book on my side of the cloth.

"What'cha doing putting a Bible in there?" Woodie asked.

"Well, that's what's put in cornerstones of churches. We can think of this buried treasure as the cornerstone to our teepee." I reasoned.

Woodie then reached inside her bag and pulled out a small metal box that once held lozenges. "This box is my secret treasure. Where is yours?"

"Already in the treasure chest."

"Where? I didn't see you put anything in other than the things you showed me."

"I hid it inside the Bible."

"You sneaky thing," she laughed. "Is that everything, now?"

"As far as I know unless you have something else," I said.

"Nope. Let's put our names and the date inside," Woodie said as she pulled a piece of paper and a pencil from her bag.

I printed: Sonja Olsen, and Woodie scribbled her name. Her handwriting was shaky, but you could read "Woodie Estes." Then I added the date: February 28, 1942.

We picked up the corners of the bandana and lifted the treasure into my metal box with our names on top, and then we folded the ends of the bandana over and put the lid on tightly.

"Woodie, you hold the box and I'll drip wax along the edges of the lid to seal it. That way water won't get in." I explained as we sat down on the ground.

"Okay!" Woodie said, the metal box shaking as she held the box up.

"Gosh! she said. "Let's rest. My arms are tired. Can't we put the box down while we're putting the wax on?"

"Sure–and get the wax mixed with dirt and leaves," I said looking around the teepee. "We need something to put on the ground." I said looking around the teepee.

"How about my bag?" Woodie asked.

"Perfect!"

So with the box on the cloth bag we dripped and dripped wax. Woodie could help with this, but I had to watch my hands and fingers because her unsteady hand shook sporadically as she tilted the lit candle.

Finally the box was completely sealed–not only the edges but all sides of the box were covered with a thick layer of wax. No water would seep into that box.

We blew out the candles and put them inside the coffee can and left the can inside the teepee.

"Woodie, do you have another sheet of paper," I asked.

"Yes, I put an extra sheet in my pocket. Why?" she responded.

"We need to make a map." I said.

"Oh, I guess you're right. Everything looks the same here." she commented.

I waited patiently while she struggled to get her boney, crooked and shaking fingers into her pocket. Finally her struggles with opening the pocket and the folded paper paid off when she produced another sheet of clean if wrinkled paper.

"Woodie, you walk off the spaces to where we will bury the treasure. I'll draw the map," I said as I unfolded the paper.

"Okay!" Woodie said.

"Start from the small oak tree next to the bridge." I instructed. "At least that won't rot away."

"Good idea, we need a landmark that will be here next year," said Woodie. She backed up to the small oak.

"Now head in the direction of the red ribbons and go straight for 10 steps. Good, now turn left. Take 10 more steps."

"Seven, eight, nine, ten," Woodie counted. "Is this the place?"

"No, next turn right and take 5 more steps. That's where we'll bury the box." I said as I placed a big X on the map.

I drew as she walked it out. "You stay right there, Woodie," I said. "I'll get the box, the knife and shovel. You get to keep the map."

"Okay," she said folding the map to put it in her pocket.

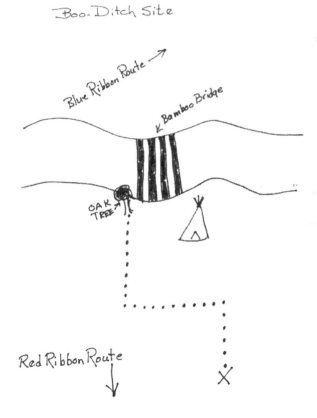

Returning, I placed the box on the ground.

"Here, Woodie. Hold the box in place while I cut around it to show where to dig."

I opened my brother's pocket knife and marked the ground. Woodie removed the box and I began slicing the roots. They were so tightly woven together that my hand got stiff and I had to stop several times to shake it out.

Finally, I'd finished. "Woodie, hand me the shovel. All those roots have been cut."

I started digging with my beach shovel. It was little, but sturdy. I dug and dug. Woodie got down on her hands and knees to pull the roots out as I dug them up.

"Don't you think that's deep enough?" Woodie asked.

"Yeah," I said wiping the sweat from my forehead. "It is."

"Here's the box," Woodie said and handed it to me.

Carefully I placed the box in the hole. There were about three inches of space in the hole above it. On our knees we started shoving the dirt over the box with our hands. Woodie worked hard, but I worked faster. We stood up and stomped the fresh soil with our feet. Finally we gathered a lot of dead bamboo leaves and scattered them over the dirt.

"Hey, Sonja," Woodie said. "Can you tell where we buried our treasure?"

"No," I said proudly. We're like the sea turtle. After laying her eggs in the sand, she camouflages it so well you can't tell the exact spot where she'd dug her nest."

"We'll be back the last Saturday in February next year to dig it up," I reminded her. "Now let's finish up. Remember, we have to dedicate this holy ground!"

Kneeling, facing each other, we said the blessing we had written while planning on the dock.

"Treasure, treasure in the ground
Hidden so good, it won't be found
No pirate, brother or Sonja's hound

Will find our treasure,
It's safe and sound."

"We've done it," we said slapping each other's palms pushing hard against each other trying to stand. But it didn't work: Woodie's legs weren't strong enough to push hard. So we fell, laughing and rolling in the leaves. I got up first and then grabbed Woodie by both hands and pulled her up.

"Remember. One year from today we will dig it up," I said.

"Let's see, "Woodie paused to think. "From the tiny oak tree at the bamboo bridge go toward the Red 10 steps. Stop. Turn left. Take 10 more steps. Stop. Turn right. Take five steps. "

"There the treasure will be buried," I said.

"Well, in case we forget. Here's the map," Woodie said.

"You keep it, Woodie," I said. My brother might find it.

I picked up the shovel as we exited through the blue ribbon path that led to the plowed field of the nursery. Emerging from the gloom of the bamboo, we were shocked by the sudden bright sunlight.

Squinting at each other, we said our good byes. Woodie turned toward her house and I walked across the field toward the back of my house.

Opening the back screen door, I called, "I'm home." No one answered. I looked out the front door and the car was gone. Mother had gone to get Daddy in Brunswick. It was Saturday and my brother and sisters were probably at the movie house.

"Good," I thought.

I took the knife to my brother's room where everything on his table was gone. 'Bet he wants to know where his knife is,' I thought. I placed the knife on the floor under the edge of the bedspread.

✧ ✧ ✧

(6)

Ditch Boo-Ditch

During spring break, Woodie and I went to Boo Ditch everyday except Sunday.

Punky followed us and was a terrible pest, always trying to get inside the teepee.

One day I lit the candle and put it on the coffee can as Punky came bouncing through the opening knocking the candle over which rolled to the croaker sack walls, which immediately caught fire.

"Woodie, grab my hand," I screamed, pulling her through the opening and leaving her just outside the teepee entrance. I ran to get help.

I raced out the blue ribbon path into the field. As luck would have it, her dad and King were hoeing in the field. "Fire! Fire! Come quick! Our teepee's on fire.!

They came running with their hoes.

"Where's Woodie?" her father demanded running into the bamboo.

"She's okay. She's out of the teepee. I made sure she got out before I ran to get you," I exclaimed.

Woodie had backed further away from the teepee and was squatting on the ground. Her arms were wrapped around her knees covered with black dirt from being dragged out of the teepee. Tears ran down her cheeks as I sat beside her, "Sssahna, our teepee. It's gone." I had been too scared to cry, but the tears started down my cheeks, too.

The Burning Hide-A-Way

King and her dad had grabbed the croaker sacks, pulled them to the ground and stomped on them. They hoed dirt over the smoldering bags and then King went back to get buckets of water to pour over the partially burned sacks.

We only had singed eyebrows...along with a lot of guilt, embarrassment and sadness that we had lost our favorite hide-a-way.

Our parents never scolded or punished us. But that was our last visit together to Boo-ditch. It's enchantment had been consumed in the fire and we never went back to recover the treasure.

✵ ✵ ✵

"Sonja, I can't believe your mother let you have matches," Will interrupted my story.

"Well, I never remember her saying anything about my not having them."

"You mean she knew you had them?" He responded in surprise.

"Sure! You don't think I'd sneak off with matches, do you? And you know that saying 'You can fool some of the people all of the time and all of the people some of the time, but you can't fool mom. You ought to know that better than anyone else."

"Remember, we lived in a world with no television, were several miles from the village, had only one car which Dad had most of time and we couldn't afford many toys. We made our own toys or improvised. When I played 'house,' my stove was a coffee can turned upside down with a lit candle under it. In our toy pots we cooked rice which never got done because we didn't have instant rice. All this was done outside in the backyard... never in the house. It was fun to use our imaginations to figure out how to do things."

"Okay! Okay! You made your point"

"Will, that little incident sure made me more careful. But it wasn't until I was older that I realized what might have happened if that fire had spread uncontrolled. That "Lovely Lane Chapel" might not be here today...Ooh, I get shivers thinking of it."

"How about the fire trucks?".

"We only had one fire truck on the island and no fire hydrants. All the water was on the truck. And everyone didn't have a telephone then. We didn't have a telephone until the war started." I explained.

"The War! What war?" Will exclaimed.

"World War II!" I replied, beginning the next part of my story.

✵ ✵ ✵

(7)

World War II

On April 8, 1942, Woodie was away in Florida. Every spring she went there for several weeks of physical therapy.

Mom had been shopping in town and stopped by the school to pick me up. My brothers and sisters would come on the school bus.

We headed for the island. As we reached the last bridge, I noticed a lot of activity at the Coast Guard Boat house, next to the bridge on the island side of the river.

"Mom, look at all those boats. What's happening? And that's Dad's boat!" I shouted.

Mother slowed down to look, even more than she usually does on a bridge and peered through the windshield. In an instant we were speeding toward the Toll House at the other end—a first for her.

I kept looking out the window. "Mom, why are all those men sitting on the ramp wrapped in blankets? They're dirty. Look at all the soldiers down there!"

"Sonja, I don't know. It looks like something awful happened and your dad's in the middle of it. I'm sure he is, if his boat is there. Do you see him?

"No."

"Watch out! There's an ambulance coming our way!"

Mother slammed on brakes while it passed us. Approaching the Toll House we saw MPs (Military Police) inspecting every car that came across the bridge.

As we were being checked, Mom leaned across the seat to the passenger window to the toll house keeper. "Mr. Chitty, what's happened?"

"A German U-boat torpedoed two ships off St. Simons early this morning. Those are the survivors down there. Your husband rescued them." he said to mother.

"What?" said mother. Her foot slipped off the clutch and brakes and the car jerked and stalled. "Oh, my gosh. Have you seen him? Is he hurt?"

"No ma'am, he isn't hurt. Just dirty and tired."

Mom started the car and sped across the road, parking on the grass.

"Come on Sonja," she said grabbing my hand, "Let's go find your Dad."

We didn't have to go far; Dad has seen us and was coming across the road. His face was black and his beard had a couple of days growth. With him was a tall man in khaki overalls, his face and overalls also streaked with dirt. Later I found out that was not all dirt; most of it was oil.

I ran ahead of mother. "Daddy, Daddy, here we are." I yelled rushing over to him.

He picked me up and gave me a hug. "Gee, you smell awful. You smell like gasoline," I said. He laughed, then put an arm around mother and gave her a big hug.

"We're okay," he reassured. "Just hungry and tired. I'll tell you all about it at the house."

"Captain Poche, this is my wife and daughter." Dad did take time for introductions.

"The captain commands one of the ships that was torpedoed. Let's go to the house, get cleaned up and some good hot coffee."

All four of us got back in the car. Dad drove with Captain Poche beside him. Mother and I were in the back seat.

When we got to the house, Mother immediately started making the coffee. "Sonja, get the cheese and cheese slicer. Here's some rye bread. Put these on the table and get the roll of salami from the refrigerator."

By the time I had put all this on the kitchen table—along with a new blue and yellow plaid oil cloth table cover, napkins, cups, saucers, spoons, knives, sugar and cream— Dad and the Captain were walking into the room.

I sat in the chair at the kitchen table. My mind was whirling with images and questions.

"Come have a seat, Captain," Dad said. Mother poured their coffee and joined us at the table.

Mom asked how dad had gotten involved.

Dad began telling his story: "I was on Cumberland Island when Mr. Ferguson of the Civil Air Patrol flew over and buzzed the house at High Point. Thinking someone was landing at the beach and signaling me to come pick them up, I ran out into the yard. But the plane kept circling and I saw something fall from the airplane. I ran to get it. It was a note attached to a wrench.

The note said, ' Two tankers torpedoed by German U-boat. Can you help pick up the survivors?' and gave the longitude and latitude. I stopped reading, got in the old truck and headed for the Cumberland wharf where the yacht was. I jumped on board the yacht, untied the ropes and took off at full speed.

When I was in St. Andrew's Sound, I took the note from my pocket and finished reading it. It said: 'If you can go, sit down in the field." Dad laughed, "Guess the pilot saw me heading for the dock and got my message. I got to St. Simons, filled the boat with gas and picked up Jesse, my sidekick, to help me."

"Taking a short cut, I beat the Coast Guard. In fact, I caught up with a State Game and Fish Boat on the way out to sea and picked up the doctor that was on board. The Coast Guard never made it. I took three life boats in tow after taking the badly injured into the yacht so they would be more comfortable and the doctor could give them first aid."

Dad laughed, "You know those Coast Guard fellers don't know the waters around here. They got lost."

Dad was a hero! Mother was relieved, glad she hadn't known about it ahead of time and that I didn't understand what all was happening.

"Captain, "Mom asked, "Were any of your crew killed?"

"Yes, but we don't know how many," he answered grimly.

I wanted to ask a lot of questions, but I would find out more if I sat there and listened to the two men talk.

"It was nighttime and that U-boat was on the surface when it fired its torpedo," the captain said.

"Why didn't the man on watch see it?" mom asked.

"Well, it was very dark. The moon wasn't shining and the submarine approached from the stern."

When Dad left to take the Captain back to his men, Mom sat down and cried. I just sat there. So much was happening to my safe, secure world. I didn't understand it all.

Things began to change after that. People whispered and I heard air raid sirens at night. The headlights on cars looked sleepy with their top half painted black to reduce the amount of light seen off shore.

Armies of military men appeared from out of the blue and the small airport became a small town overnight with barracks, hangers and rows of fighter planes, their wings folded up. Odd things kept washing up on the beach– oranges, cabbages, and mattresses from the sunken ships at first. Then bodies from patrol planes that had been shot down by surfaced U-boats, and parts of airplanes.

People arrived from the farms in droves to work at the shipyard. Schools were so overcrowded we attended in shifts. Every time a ship was launched at the shipyard, the marsh for miles around acquired an even layer of oily wax they used to grease the rails.

The day after Woodie got home from Florida she came to my house very excited. "Sonja! I heard about your dad seeing the German submarine! Did they shoot at him?"

I had to chuckle. "No, Woodie, he never saw any Germans or a U-boat--that's what they call German submarines."

"Well hurry up and tell me what did happen!"

"It's what still might happen that scares me," I said. "U-boats are sinking our ships, and people say that spies are being brought on shore at night. What if we actually met one around here--what would we do?"

"Yeah, that's scary. But what about your dad?"

"He was asked to pick up the sailors who weren't killed when the torpedo struck their ship and had gotten into lifeboats," I explained proudly. "You know Woodie, he never acted scared when I saw him. But even if he was, he didn't think twice about heading out to sea to pick up those survivors!"

"That's what he did? He rescued the survivors?"

"Yep! That's my Dad!"

Woodie knew I adored my dad and always considered it a treat to go along with him on his yacht--it wasn't really his, but since he was the captain we thought it was.

Mom couldn't swim and was afraid of the water, like she was afraid of snakes.

Dad wasn't afraid of anything, at least as far as I knew. He was always plunging into something and showing he wasn't weak.

Dad's always active mind was the real source of his strength. He could think through almost any situation or problem, and either solve it or take the first steps toward a solution.

And Dad never minced words. I remember watching him back the yacht into a slip at the dock, and if anyone happened to be standing in his sight line he wouldn't politely ask them to move; oh, no. He'd shout "Get away from the door!" But then he always docked the yacht perfectly.

Daddy always wanted me to learn about boats, although Mom preferred that I sit on the dock and fish rather than do something more exciting with Dad. But Dad would get me to do things so I'd learn about boats.

"Sonja," I remember him saying one day as we cruised up the river, "go to the bow and curl that rope so it doesn't fall into the water." Mom would be cringing in the cabin as she watched me tiptoe up the edge of the deck around the cabin to the bow.

Once sitting on the bow and curling the rope oh so carefully, so proudly, I could hear Mom chastising Dad for sending me out there. Dad just laughed. That sound was as tasty as the salt spray and reminded me of the sense of trust and encouragement that Dad gave me.

Then one day I could walk to the bow without even holding the little railing on the top of the cabin...a real accomplishment but also a tiny act of defiance.

(8)

Fishing Alone

During the war, in front of our house, gasoline was pumped into trucks from a barge at the dock where I fished. The hubbub of trucks transporting loads of gasoline to the airport, crunching the shells on the road all day and night, and the lights at night shining into our bedroom windows are images I would never forget.

But after a while, Woodie and I stopped talking about the war or spies.

Once we had gotten used to all the war production activity in and around the island, life on our road seemed to remain normal. Except about every three months when they pumped gasoline into the trucks from the barge. But that was about all that affected us.

I loved the solitude and quietness of our part of the island and doing things by myself. I enjoyed becoming more resourceful like dad. This was best done alone when I could think without having to be on the alert because of Woodie's handicap.

There were two docks at the river, the county one and the old Boat Club dock. The county dock extended a good distance over the water and had a railing.

Mother never questioned my solo trips to the dock to fish and crab. I liked to use live shrimp for bait because they helped me catch trout and bass and flounder.

But, I started out with nothing, except my ingenious, clever, and increasingly analytical mind!

From the top of the bluff I could look down at the fiddler crabs basking in the sun outside their holes in the muddy sand. I didn't have a cast net to catch shrimp and had to start somewhere. I knew that sheepshead like a certain kind of fiddler; the kind that had gray oval-shaped shells with iridescent colors...the males with one big claw and one small claw; the females with two small claws. If they pinched your finger, it hurt! That was the fiddler I watched in silence.

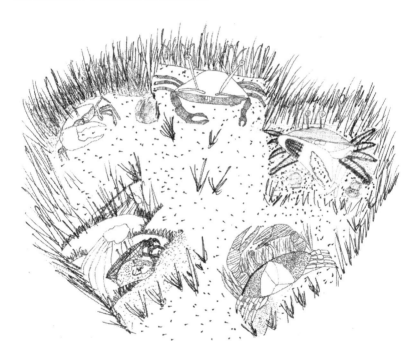

In one hand I had a rusty coffee can with sand and in the other a short flat pointed stick. I scurried down to make my attack, because the moment they felt the earthquake from my running, they'd disappeared into their holes. However, they went in just far enough to be out of sight, so if I poked my stick in back of the hole the fiddler dashed out. I was waiting with my grubby hand to catch this bait–the first step to catching lots of fish.

Once I had ten or eleven fiddlers burrowing into the sand in my rusty coffee can, I was ready. Since I was going to do more than fish, I went down on the county dock.

My fishing rig was a hand line I made with fishing cord, two hooks and a sinker. First I baited the two hooks, threading lengthwise through the fiddler's body.

Then I dropped the fishing line into the water next to a piling encrusted with oysters and barnacles. I knew sheepshead feed on those little suckers! When I felt a nibble, I jerked on the line. Sheepshead are tricky and don't get caught on the first or second nibble. But I know when it's a sheepshead nibbling because they eat everything except the shell.

After many nibbles, I'd hook a sheepshead. There's nothing so exciting as feeling that jerk as I hand over hand pulled the line to the surface with a sheepshead on my hook.

For the next step in my fishing chain I'd catch a crab. I cut off the head of the sheepshead using it for crab bait. I tied it into a crab basket and put the basket in the water.

Next I'd use a homemade shrimp net that Mother crocheted with fine thread; a circle three feet in diameter. I sewed the edges to a large round piece of iron, making a shallow net with no top. In the bottom of the net I tied a weight. Most of the time I used a lead elbow pipe for the weight. Sinkers cost money. Besides there were all sorts of lead pipes in the workshop.

I tied four pieces of cord two feet long evenly spaced to the iron ring, brought the ends together and tied them together, so the net was balanced. To this I attached a line long enough to reach from the dock to the bottom of the river. My first crab would be smashed and tied into the shrimp net.

Catching shrimp is tricky! They are always jumping when they come out of the water, and can swim through a net if the holes are big. If you bring the net up too fast, the shrimp will swim out before you get it out of the water.

The trick is to get the net out of the water as smoothly as possible. Slowly, inch by inch, hand over hand, I pull up the net. As soon as the rim was out of the water the shrimp began jumping, so the speed of pulling increased. Once the net reached the dock, I caught the hopping shrimp and put them into a bucket of sea water.

Now I had several things going on. I fished for trout, bass, flounders or croakers with the shrimp. With the rest of the fiddlers I caught more sheepshead. I had a crab basket catching crabs, in the shrimp net I caught small shrimp for bait and to eat.

It kept me busy going from one operation to the other, but provided our family with many seafood platters. How proud I was to have ingeniously used my mind starting from nothing and coming home the bread winner! My brother wasn't the only genius in the family!

One fateful day about a month after the ships were sunk I was well into my multi-tasked fishing on the county dock when I saw something floating toward the dock on the incoming tide. It looked like a small brown chest, about a foot long and eight or nine inches wide.

It floated into the marsh by the dock and stopped. I wanted to retrieve it before the current got stronger and pushed it out of the marsh. But how? If only I had a cast net, I could cast over it and bring it in.

I couldn't walk out into the marsh from the shore without getting bogged down to my waist in mud. I was not allowed to go out in a boat by myself. But I could tie a boat to the dock ladder. Would the rope be long enough to reach the box?

My eyes glanced over to the wooden rowboat on the edge of the water. It belonged to Cleansie, a man who lived up the road. Maybe he wouldn't mind my using it, if I put it back and tied it up good.

I hurriedly arrived at a plan. First I had to push the boat into the water and paddle it across "open water" to the dock. If the boat was sitting on slippery mud and not sand, I might could push it. I would be safe since the water was shallow and the current was not strong close to shore.

Of course, I wouldn't tell mom.

The boat was heavy, its stern was in the mud where it was slick. The bow was on the sand so I had to try to pick up the bow.

Impossible--it was too heavy. So I stood in the stern and rocked the boat back and forth. Inch by inch the boat began to move in the mud and soon the stern reached the water and the bow was now in the mud. I got out and pushed on the bow until the whole boat was in the water.

I slipped in the mud several times, once hitting my chin on the bow of the boat. My feet, legs and clothes were covered with mud, my chin hurt and I was sweating heavily.

As I stepped into the boat I slipped from all the mud on my feet and hit my elbow on the seat. My injuries hurt and at some skinned places on my legs there was blood mixed with the mud.

But I had to get that box! No time to worry about a little blood. It looked like a treasure chest that I was determined to get. I'd worry later about mother seeing my injuries.

I managed to paddle the boat up to the ladder on the other side of the dock. Grasping the rope, I tied one end to the lowest rung of the ladder and the other end to the cleat on the bow. I pushed away from the dock with the stern headed toward the box.

The rope was stretched out all the way, but I was still about two feet from the box and the boat kept drifting back toward the dock on the tide. I kept paddling toward the box, but had to figure out a way to reach the box and get it to the boat.

In the bottom of the boat was an old wet muddy dress shirt with long sleeves, and a fishing line. I unwound the line, put the hook into one of the long sleeves, and shook out the shirt so it would cover a bigger space when I threw it over the box. If I threw it like a cast net, it might cover the box and I could slowly draw the fishing line back in with the box. I didn't own a cast net, but had watched people cast.

The boat had drifted back to the dock so I paddled out again until the rope was completely stretched. Then I dropped the paddles in the boat, stood on the stick that held the fishing line. Then I proceeded with the great cast of all times...

I hoped!

I picked up the shirt, holding one edge of it in my teeth; the bottom of the edge of the back was in my left hand and the edge of the bottom of the other front in the other hand. Then twisting my whole body, my arms outstretched, I hurled the shirt through the air.

Spreading like a parachute, it landed on top of the box. My first cast had worked and the wet shirt clung to the box. I was careful not to pull real hard or jerk it and the box floated toward me as I pulled in the line. When it was within reach, I let go of the line and reached over the stern to lift the box in the boat. It was not as light as I thought it would be. I got on my knees on the back seat and leaned over, grabbing the handle on one end and pulling the box into the boat. On the top of the box was a small brass plate that read **SS Baton Rouge, ABS Watson.**[*] This had come off one of the torpedoed ships!

All of a sudden the boat hit the dock and I was jolted over into the bottom of the boat. Engrossed in studying the box, I hadn't realized the tide was moving the boat. Now I had another bruise to explain to mother.

My body was sore all over, but I had to get on with my task. I untied the rope from the ladder, paddled under the dock to land the boat where I had found it. I couldn't get it as far up onto land as before, but tied the rope to a tree. Unhooking the fishing line from the shirt, I rolled up the line and put the shirt back in the bottom of the boat.

I struggled getting the heavy box out of the boat and once on land, I tried to open the box; but it was locked. Having lost my interest in fishing, I threw all the shrimp, crabs and sheepshead I had caught overboard. I could catch them another day.

All my fishing tackle was put away in the bucket. But to carry the shrimp net, the crab basket, bucket and the box was impossible so I hid all my fishing gear under the dock in the grass where the tide didn't come and nobody could see it. I headed to the house, dragging the box by the handle.

Before long the box lay inside the moss covered chair hide-a-way in the front yard. Thank goodness no one was home; it was Saturday Matinee time, so my brother was engrossed in cowboy exploits. I wasn't interested in cowboys. My sisters were visiting friends. Dad was on Cumberland and Mom was grocery shopping on the mainland and waiting to pick up my other siblings about 5 p.m. On Saturdays I stayed home.

Taking off my muddy clothes, I washed myself off with the hose, left the clothes on the ground, dried my feet on the door mat as best I could and went inside. I took a quick bath, poured alcohol on my scrapes and put on clean clothes.

---

* Able Bodied Seaman

Then hunting through my brother's room, I found his keys–all sorts of keys. I hurried outside and crawled into *Mossy Chairs*, took out the keys and tried key after key but couldn't get the box opened.

No one could know about my discovery. It was my find and mine alone. So I decided to go to Boo-Ditch and bury it. This would be my secret and some day I could recover and open it. I wondered what treasures could be inside.

My brother's keys went back to his room. Then from the garage I got my wagon, put the big shovel, and the box in it and ventured down the road to Boo Ditch.

It felt strange going back into the bamboo after the fire, but no one was around to see me go in. Woodie and her parents always shopped on Saturday afternoons and didn't get home until after supper.

I got to the bridge and from the oak tree measured off my steps, but this time I went in the opposite direction from our buried treasure. I dug and dug. The shovel was sharp and cut through the roots much more easily than when I had a pocket knife. This box needed a hole much bigger than the one I had dug for our tin. Finally the hole was big enough for the box so I put it in, covered it with dirt and leaves and headed back to the dock with the wagon.

I put all the fishing gear in the wagon and carried it home. No one was home yet, so I put up the fishing gear, wagon and shovel, rinsed my dirty clothes well with the hose and hung them on the line. Then I waited for everyone else to come home.

When mother questioned me about my scrapes and bruises, I said I was running down the shell road, tripped and fell. She believed me–I think!

✵ ✵ ✵

(9)

Shelling The Road

Being summertime, Woodie and I played outside everyday it wasn't raining. On some rainy days we played 'school' with my sister, Cecilia. She was our teacher.

One rainy day we played 'store' on Woodie's screened porch. Our money was the green leaves from the plants her mother had on the porch. We were rich by the time we'd stripped the plants clean of those dollar bills! Needless to say, we never did that again after her mother discovered her leafless plants, scolded us and sent me home.

Sometimes I got tired of playing with Woodie. We always played 'ball' and I was always giving in to her in any game of challenge "just because she wasn't right!"

Woodie had all kinds of balls she threw to strengthen her muscles and improve her coordination. In fact, I got tired of playing "ball" with her. Throwing the ball back and forth; throwing the ball against the house; throwing the ball at a tennis racket. Ugh!

When I got so tired of throwing the ball up against the concrete steps, I'd hurl it over their roof and into their backyard instead. It would become a game, running around the house to find the ball and running back to resume the familiar 'ball.'

Unknowingly, I was Woodie's physical therapist.

Today we were taking our "school" books into the *Mossy Chairs* where it was cooler.

"Sonja! Come here a minute." Mother called.

"Gee, Woodie, what does she want now? We just got settled in." I complained. "Wait here. I'll see what she wants."

So I crawled out from my cubby hole between the arms of one of the over-turned wooden lawn chairs and ran to the house. Mother was standing on the porch.

"Sonja, you're gonna itch all over from those chiggers in that moss," mother said pulling a silver-gray tendril from my hair.

"What's the matter?" I asked ignoring her comment.

"Nothing's the matter, Sonja, I owe Rosalie some money for washing and ironing. I thought you and Woodie might like to take it to her," mother said reaching down giving me a little hit on my behind for being so sassy.

"Sure." I said changing the tone of my voice. "Where is it?"

I hated to leave our mossy house, but now Woodie and I might get a chance to play with Willie Mae and Fannie, Rosalie's granddaughters. And better yet, hear one of Rosalie's stories.

"You get Woodie and I'll have it ready for you," mother said.

I ran back to the mossy house and stuck my head in through the silver thread-like covering. "Come on, Woodie. Mother wants us to take Rosalie some money," I said. "Maybe Willie Mae and Fannie will be there and we can play with them a while."

"Sure, let's get going," Woodie slurred as she moved slowly on her knees through the opening.

"Don't tell mother we want to stay and play. We'll just do it anyway." I schemed.

Rosalie lived up the shell road from us in Jewtown, a section of the island that had been settled by the freed slaves after the Civil War. The name "Jew Town" was given to it during sawmill days when two Jewish merchants, Sig and Robert Levison, owned and operated a general store there. They called it Levisonville, but that was too hard to pronounce, so they it became known as "Jewtown."

Brushing off the sand, leaves and bits of moss, we hurried to the house. Mother met us at the screen door and handed me an envelope.

Woodie and I ambled along the oyster shell road leading to Rosalie's house kicking bits of shells and stirring up the white chalky dust.

"Bet I can throw further than you can," I said eyeing the broken shells that paved the road.

"Bet you can't," Woodie challenged. "I throw balls all the time."

How true!

"O.K. We'll see." I said. "Let me get you a shell." I stooped down with my backside toward Woodie. I didn't want her to see how carefully I was choosing her shell.

"Here, Woodie. Here's a nice shell. Who's first?"

"I'll go first," Woodie said taking the shell that I had selected with her shaky boney fingers. Pulling her arm back over her head and tottering as she struggled to give the swing all her might, she chucked the shell through the air. It floated in a high arc and landed on the road without skips or hops. It had gone a long way.

Woodie shuffled quickly to mark the place. "Your turn now," she called.

"Move over. I don't want to hit you," I said as I pitched my carefully chosen shell. It soared through the air hitting the ground with a bump, bump, bumpity, bump. Each bump carrying it further down the road.

"Where did it land?" I asked.

"Oh, it's about three feet beyond mine," Woodie said with disgust as she stomped unevenly over to my shell.

"You always win. You're stronger than me. That's not fair."

"No, I'm just smarter." I joked as I ran to see where my shell landed. No sooner had I gotten the words out of my mouth than I realized I shouldn't have said them. Feeling bad about what I had said but not for outwitting her, I confessed. "I just used a heavier shell. The shell I gave you was light and floated up; then when it hit the ground, it stayed in one place."

Wanting to redeem myself, I said, "I bet if we try again we'll throw about the same distance"

"This time," Woodie retorted. "We'll use the same shell!"

So we squatted in the middle of the road searching for the right shell.

"Here's a heavy one," I said "Do you want to use it?"

"It's okay," she said as her crooked fingers took it from the palm of my hand.

Taking turns throwing from the same place, we drew a line in the road where the shell landed. Sometimes her shell went further. Sometimes mine did and I threw with all my might each time.

By the time we'd shelled our way to Rosalie's, Woodie was boasting about how many times she beat me. Any hurt feelings had been forgotten. We were friends!

✧ ✧ ✧

(10)

ROSALIE'S

"Look, Sonja. There's Willie Mae and Fannie." Woodie shouted excitedly as she began running toward Rosalie's house.

"Yippee!" I exclaimed. "We'll get to play."

Rosalie's granddaughters' heads bobbed up and down over the wooden fence. Willie Mae had a red bow on the top of her hair and Fannie a white one. As we pushed open the rickety gate, we saw they were playing hopscotch on the clean swept black dirt yard in front of Rosalie's home.

Rosalie's cabin was on the edge of the settlement inhabited by descendants of the island's plantation slaves. It seemed as old as the live oak tree in her front yard. Rosalie's cabin was topped with a rusting tin roof, and the weathered gray boards on the sides might have been waiting for a tap to send them slapping to the ground.

The porch roof slanted toward the ground on one end, where its support post had slipped down. The front outside walls were sided with rusty metal signs advertising Coca Cola, R. C. Cola, and Camel cigarettes. The windows and doorframe were painted a robin's egg blue to keep out the 'haints.' One wondered if the color, now faint from weathering was strong enough to keep the haints out.

Rosalie stood on the porch, her arms arched on each side of her hips. The eyes in her turbaned head smiled through the smoke from her corn cob pipe. Walking up to her, I extended my

59

hand with the envelope. "Here's the money mom owes you." I said. As she was reaching for it, Fannie called out, "Let's play hide and seek. Not IT."

Willie Mae and Woodie each quickly shouted, "Not IT."

I was IT.

Home base was the chopping block underneath the huge oak with its heavy low hanging limbs.

"Ten, twenty, thirty, forty, fifty, sixty, seventy, eighty, ninety, one hundred," I counted slowly, pausing between numbers so I could listen for footsteps.

The only thing I heard other than two steps that seemed to go in opposite directions was the squawking of Blue Jays.

I shouted, "Coming. Ready or not." Puzzled, I opened my eyes, squinting to adjust to the light. I walked to the corner of the house. Rosalie sat on the porch rocking, her head leaning on the back of the chair and her eyes apparently closed. I saw the leaves of the oleander bush jiggling. "I spy, Woodie behind the oleander bush," I yelled, racing to the chopping block.

In the middle of the yard was the huge black witch's cauldron that Rosalie used to boil laundry. Willie Mae's red ribbon hair bow was showing over its top. "I spy Willie Mae behind the witch's pot," I said and turned to run to the chopping block. To my surprise, Fannie was sitting on the block. I had not heard her run or seen her. Where had she been?, I wondered. They all started to laugh.

"Fooled you, didn't I," Fannie boasted.

We had several good places to hide. The oleander bushes lined along one side of the house were easy to slip behind. You just had to make sure the leaves didn't move. A broken-down fence covered with honeysuckle vines stood at one end of the yard and in the middle of the dirt yard was the black cauldron. Now I was about to find out about another good hiding place.

"Where were you?" I demanded. "I thought I knew all the hiding places."

"Well," confessed Fannie. "I climbed up the big old oak tree and hid behind the big blobs of moss. When you weren't looking I crawled out on the low limb hanging over the chopping block and slid down when your back was turned.

We kept on hiding and seeking. Each one trying to get up in the tree first.

Finally Woodie said, "It's not fair. "I can't climb that tree by myself."

"Oh, you chilins, you make an ol' woman tired," a voice from the rocking chair grunted. I bet I know a tree not one of young'uns's would hide in!"

"Where is it?" Woodie asked.

"Along side de road you jist walked up," replied Rosalie.

"I bet I'd climb it," said Fannie.

"Me, too." chimed in Willie Mae.

"Come on, Rosalie," I pleaded. "Why do you think we wouldn't hide in it?"

(11)

The Nail and Stob

As the girls huddled in high expectation at her feet, Rosalie rested her turbaned head on the back of her chair and started.

"Many years ago dar wuz a cotton plantation whar Sonja and Woodie live. De owner had many slaves. But dar wuz one who wuz young and strong. His name wuz Primus. Primus wuz de massa's mos' trusted slave. On de same plantation wuz a slave girl named Renda. Renda wuz de mistress's 'mos trusted house slave. Primus and Renda luved each other. One day Primus approached de massa. "Massa," he sed. "I's in love with Renda. Would you give me 'mission to marry her?"

"Well, Primus," de massa sed thinkin' of all de strong chil'ns they'd have, "Sure."

"Anoder thin', massa," Primus continued. "Do you think you'd eber sep'rate us by sellin' us to diff'nt massas?"

De massa looked straight into Primus' eyes as if testin' his honor. Primus stared back never flinchin'. Convinced his intent wuz worthy, he sed, "Primus, I'll never sep'rate you. But you'll have to be married by de black preacher. He won't be here for a month. I'm goin' Nor' tomorrow to find a buyer for de cotton, but I'll be back before he comes."

"Thanks ya, massa!" Primus sed bowin' and grinnin' from ear to ear showin' his bright white teeth.

Now de massa's son had returned several months earlier to de plantation after bein' up Nor' fer six years gettin' a book learnin' ed'cation. That's not all de ed'cation he got up Nor'. He got an ed'cation in gamblin'.

Because his fader wuz wealthy, he thought he could do anythin' he wanted. De plantation gave him a place to sleep, good food to eat and slaves to obey him. He eben wuz paid to ride with de overseer to see how to manage de plantation. But when his fader found out about his gamblin' up Nor', he warned his son that if he eber gambled again, he'd dis'herit him and banish him from de plantation.

He didn't heed his fader's warnin' and soon wuz in debt to de meanest sea wolves ever to come into de port. He didn't have de money to pay. He knew what would happened to him if his fader found out. And he knew that dese men would beat him, if he didn't come up wid de money. He wuz between a rock and a hard place. He spent many a-night thinkin' how he could get a lot of money. Time wuz runnin' out for him. Den de idea came to him to sell one of his fader's slaves. Renda and Primus would brin' de most money. Primus wuz too strong for him. Renda wuz de one he would sell.

He made a deal with a slave trader on de mainland. His fader's trip up Nor' came just in time.

It wuz a moonless night when de son sneaked into Renda's cabin. Gaggin her, he dragged her to de river. He wuz meetin' de slave trader that wuz comin' to de landin' on Hawkins Crick.

That same night Primus wuz down on de crick a-flounder giggin'. When he heard water drippin' in a steady rhythm, he knew that someone wuz rowin' in de crick. He kneeled down on de muddy shoreline and peered though de marsh grass.

What he saw made his heart sick. De gleam from de son's lantern show'd Renda strugglin' as de son pulled her toward de landin'. Primus ran out on de dock to free her, but wuz whacked on de head with an oar by one of de oarsmen. He fell with a thud off de dock into de marsh grass. He didn't wake up 'til daybreak.

De next mornin' Renda wuz missin'. A search wuz made of all de cabins. Dey didn't find Renda, but dey found one of her dresses in Primus' cabin under his cot. It wuz soaked with blood.

Afraid that Primus would tell his fader what happened, de massa's son planted de idea that Renda had been murdered by Primus 'cause she'd fallen in love with someone else. De son took one of Renda's dresses and proceeded to dip it in chicken blood. He had hidden it that night in Primus' cabin.

Before de fader came home, de son convinced de overseer that Primus wuz guilty.

Rosalie stopped.

She looked at us girls and said, You know that big ol' oak tree on de road a-comin' here?

We all nodded in silence. "Has you ev'r seen de nail and stob on it."

Looking puzzled we said in unison, "What's a stob?"

"It's a short flat piece of wood." Rosalie explained.

"Oooh" they all sighed realizing they had seen the nail and stob many times.

"Well," Rosalie said eerily, "dey hung Primus."

We all gasped together, "Who hung him?"

"De overseer and de massa's son," Rosalie said sadly. "Dey hung him from that tree one evenin' at dusk. Dey tied Primus up, put a noose around his neck and sat him on a horse. Den de overseer climbed up in de tree, twisted de rope 'round that stob and nailed it high on de tree. De son gave de horse a whack on his rump and..."

Not one word that Rosalie uttered went past our ears.

"It's sed that on moonless nights Primus walks up'n down de road lookin' for his sweetheart." Rosalie said.

Woodie and I left Rosalie's house with a haunting feeling as the sun's last rays disappeared behind the trees. "Do you believe that story? Do you think that man was hung on that tree?" Woodie asked.

Nail and Stob

"I've seen the nail and stob on the tree. It's way up high," I said, voice quivering as we picked up our pace.

"There it is!" said Woodie pointing up to the tree. They could barely see the stob with dusk folding in around.

All of a sudden Woodie stopped. "Look, Sonja. See that light?" she whispered as a bright cloud-like image floated from the underbrush behind the tree.

"No, I don't see anything," I said, trying to sound brave. "Come on, let's get home. We're already late for supper."

As Woodie peered into the shadows she said, "Sonja! The light is beginning to look like a person. It must be Primus, the slave Rosalie was telling us about!"

"How do you know?" I said strongly. The fading light of day outlined the trees and bushes creating all kinds of imaginary creatures. "I don't see anything except the shadows of the trees.

The tentacles of moss hanging from the branches was scary enough for me without having to look for a ghost.

"He's coming closer. Look! I see his big bare feet! Listen! I hear something," exclaimed Woodie. "Sounds like he's weeping," she murmured. "His head is bent toward the ground. And look, he's heading toward the river."

I grabbed Woodie's hand and pulled her back. "Wait a minute. Don't go so fast. We don't want to run into something I can't see."

Woodie always had an unsteady gait, but now she was shaking all over. Her voice was more slurred than usual when she said, "He turned around. He's looking at us. There's no place to hide!"

"Oh, my gosh," I stammered. "I see him."

Woodie and I clung frozen to each other in the middle of the road, our eyes glued to the figure floating toward the river in front of us. The faint pink glow in the western sky faded to a gray gloom as the vision sank into the marsh.

The appearance of the headlights of a car coming down the road brought us back to our senses. Holding Woodie's boney hand I started running pulling her as fast as I could toward my house.

"Where have you girls been?" Mother queried, rather irritated when she heard the screen door squeak on its hinges as we sneaked into the house. "Woodie, your mother is looking for you."

"We stayed at Rosalie's house and played with Willie Mae and Fannie," Woodie faintly confessed.

"We were having so much fun, we forgot to look at the clock. We're out of breath because we knew we were late." I lied.

"Well, Sonja. That's no excuse. You should have been watching the sun. It's almost dark. You will have to walk Woodie home and come back by yourself. Next time keep an eye on the sun. I feel like punishing you good."

Picking up the flashlight as we walked out the door, I whispered to Woodie "Punishment! It'll be punishment enough to have to walk home alone in the dark. Primus might decide to come out of the marsh and meet me on the way back."

"I'm sorry," said Woodie holding my hand as we followed the gleam of light. "Dad could have come for me. They are trying to teach us a lesson. Guess they have succeeded."

"But we've got one on them," I said. "They've never seen the ghost and we have. It's our secret." We both agreed. We never did even talk about it again. And we never walked up that road again in the late afternoon.

(12)

Shall We Gather At the River?

On a late Sunday afternoon during the summer, Woodie and I were in the yard adding moss to the top of our lawn-chair hideaway.

"What's that?" I said.

"What's what?" Woodie asked.

"I thought I heard a crunching sound from the road that led to Jew Town."

"A crunching sound! I don't hear anything." Woodie said.

"Be still." I insisted. We froze to listen.

The sound got louder.

"Something's coming down that road!" I said. "And it ain't a car. You think it's Primus?"

"Those oyster shells are being crunched by something big, and Primus only comes out at dusk," Woodie noted.

"Woodie, let's go look," I said grabbing her hand and pulling her to the road.

"What in the world!" Woodie exclaimed.

Coming down the road was what looked like the whole population of Jew Town. Some were swaying in a slow steady rhythm as they headed toward the river as if keeping in time to music. Others were loaded into a wagon drawn by a slow pulling mule. The only sound was the crunching of the oyster shells as the wheels turned. No one said a word.

"There's going to be a baptism!" I whispered.

"A baptism! Where?"

"Shhh! Not so loud. At the river, dummy! You need water to be baptized. Jesus was baptized in a river. See those people dressed in white sheets." I said pointing to the procession. "They are going to be baptized. I've seen it before. They come down to the river ever so often to baptize." I continued. "They always come on a Sunday afternoon when the tide is high...cold or hot weather."

It must of been the whole St. Paul's Missionary Baptist congregation from Jew Town.

Not wanting to cause a distraction, Woodie and I sat down Indian style beside an oleander tree in the yard and watched as the congregation grew closer.

"Look!" Woodie said as she pointed to the crowd. I jerked her hand down. She was pointing to two young girls dressed in white sheet robes. "It's Willie Mae and Fannie. They're going to be baptized!"

"Yeah," I whispered," but don't talk so loud and don't point.

Becoming more excited Woodie pointed again. "I see Rosalie and her daughters, Lavinia Belle, Maebelle, and Elizabeth Belle. That must be King's wife with him."

"Oh, my, there's James with his second wife and young'uns. Remember we saw them one day crabbing at the dock." Sonja added.

"Yeah, what was it she said to her stepchildren?" Woodie asked.

"The stepdaughter said something about toting the crab basket and her stepmother said, 'Don't say tote, say carry'." Sonja giggled.

"Then the stepson said, 'That ain't the way to do it' and the stepmother said, 'Don't say 'ain't', say 'isn't'." Woodie said finishing the episode. "Seems as though we got a lesson in good grammar right at the dock."

"There's old Magwood." I whispered into Woodie's ear. "The one with a long white beard. He should be riding in the wagon." Magwood, using his walking cane, struggled to keep up with the others. His legs were bowed from old age, but his face shone with joy. Magwood had been a good friend of my grandparents when they lived at the sawmill. I had been in the car when we took grandma to visit him one time.

Leading the procession was the preacher dressed in his black robes carrying a Bible under his arm. He was tall and stately. His manner was ceremonious. Beside him was a man carrying a long stick. "That's Cleansie," I whispered. "The one with the stick."

After they passed us, we followed them to the river, but stayed up on the bluff under a cedar tree and watched as they gathered beside the river.

The tide was high; the water smooth and clear. The only sounds were a marsh hen trilling in the marsh grass and the hum of flies around a dead fish on the dock.

Cleansie walked out into the water. "Oh, I know what the stick is for," I whispered. "He is measuring the depth of the water." When he got to the right depth, he stopped and hammered the stick into the sand beneath the water.

As if God was the choir director bringing in the chorus, the crowd started singing together, *Gonna lay down my sword and shield, down by the riverside, down by the riverside, down by the riverside. Gonna lay down my sword and shield down by the riverside. Ain't gonna study war no more. Ain't gonna study war no more, ain't gonna study war no more, ain't gonna study war no more.*

"Gosh, there's a lot of "ain'ts" in that song" Woodie said. "It can't be wrong."

They continued singing. *I'm gonna lay down my heavy load, down by the riverside, down by the riverside, down by the riverside...*

Then another verse: *I'm gonna lay down my travelin' shoes down by the riverside...*

By this time I started singing with them even though I didn't know how each verse started, but once I heard it, I sang.

"I'm gonna put on my long white robe down by the riverside..."

"Well," interrupted Woodie, "I wondered when they were gonna get to the baptism and the white robes. I guess that is all the verses now."

It wasn't and I continued to sing: *"Gonna put on that starry crown down by the riverside..."*

"What did you say?" I snickered. "Last verse?" Woodie made me so mad sometimes. Just because she had trouble saying and singing words was no excuse for her to not want me to sing.

"Okay," she said, "there are more verses. I just thought when they got to the 'long white robes' they had gotten to baptism time. That's all."

The singing continued. I sang louder: *"I'm gonna walk with that Prince of Peace down by the riverside, down by the riverside...*

The singing stopped and the preacher stepped out in front and read from the Bible. "And it came to pass in those days, that Jesus came from Nazareth of Galilee, and was baptized of John in the Jordan River. And straightway coming up out of the water, he saw the heavens opened, and the Spirit like a dove descending upon him: And there came a voice from heaven, saying, Thou art my beloved Son, in whom I am well pleased." Mark 1:9-11.

Those robed in white followed the preacher to the water's edge. The congregation all at one time without a director started singing, *"Wade in the water, wade in the water, children, wade in the water God's a-going to trouble the water. See that host all dressed in white, God's a-going to trouble the water. The leader looks like an Israelite. God's a-going to trouble the water."*

The singing stopped, those dressed in white stood at the water's edge. The preacher said: "Let us pray."

"Bow your head, Woodie," I said.

"Why?"

"Because he's praying. When you pray you bow your head and close your eyes to think about what the preacher is praying. That way God gets the message."

"Okay." Woodie said as she bowed her head.

Then we heard the prayer come forth with a booming voice. It wasn't the preacher. Woodie and I looked up at the same time. It was Magwood. We bowed our heads again to listen.

"O, Fader, God in heav'n, hear us your servants. We're here today to bring into your fold by the water of ba'tism your children."

At that point someone from the congregation said... "Amen." But he continued and continued and continued praying and the "Amens" kept a-coming.

"My neck is hurting," complained Woodie. "I agree with all those people who kept saying "Amen"...It was time for that prayer to end."

"Shhh," I hissed. "Amen means 'so be it.' They are just agreeing with him. Now be quiet. It won't hurt you to listen for a change."

Magwood kept on going and going and finally he said, "Lord, we thank you and we ask you to bless des chilins' here today. Amen."

"Whew!" said Woodie as she stretched her neck, "that's one 'Amen' I was glad to hear!"

"Me, too," I admitted.

"Look, Willie Mae is going into the water." Woodie said.

The preacher was wading in the water followed by Cleansie leading Willie Mae. They stopped in front of the stick. The pastor grabbed Willie Mae's nose and put his hand over her mouth and said "I baptize you in the name of Father," and dunked her head backwards into the river... "and the Son" and dunked her again... "and the Holy Ghost. Amen." and he dunked her the third time backwards into the water.

"Gosh, I am glad I was baptized with a few drops of water when I was a baby," I said. "I thought he was going to drown her bending her backwards."

"Me, too," said Woodie staring at the soaking wet Willie Mae.

Then it was Fannie's turn. Finally, the last one was baptized and they all stood on the shore in dripping white sheets.

"I know it's summer," Woodie said, "but I believe they are cold."

"Look, they are shivering," I said.

"Are they going home in those wet robes?" Woodie asked. The answer came immediately as everyone turned and started back up the road. This time they weren't silent. They broke out in song.

Joyful hands began clapping and the movement speeded up. Shouts of "hallelujahs" rang through the air. They walked faster than on the way down. Willie Mae and Fannie led the group.

"I bet they are going fast and clapping and singing to keep warm." Woodie said as Willie Mae and Fannie waved at us. We waved back.

It was getting late. "So much for re-mossing our hide-a-way." I said.

"Yeah," said Woodie, and it's time for supper. See you later."

As she walked crookedly down the road, I went into the house thinking about what the preacher read when Jesus was baptized. "This is my beloved Son in whom I am well pleased." If God was pleased for his Son to be baptized, surely he is pleased with all of us who were baptized.

74

(13)

Back to Reality

As we approached the island, Will exclaimed, "Look, Sonja, there are the bridges! But they are concrete!" There was a sad tone to his voice as he continued. "Where are the wooden ones?"

"They were replaced back in the 40s after World War II. This is the second set of concrete bridge and there isn't a Mr. Chitty there anymore to open the bridge for boats. The bridges are high enough for boats to go under" I explained. "Also, we don't pay toll anymore," I added.

"Look to your left," I gestured as we were crossing the last bridge. "That's where I grew up. I'll take you there after the funeral. First we'll head on up to Christ Church, since it is almost 3 o'clock and we don't want to be late."

The ceremony in the cemetery was very short. After the family left, Charlie approached me,

"Sonja, can you come by the house? I have read Woodie's will and there was a sealed envelope addressed to you folded inside the will."

"My goodness," I said. "What in the world has Woodie got in an envelope for me?"

At the house Charlie gave me the envelope and written in Woodie's shaky handwriting was my name, 'Sonja.' I nervously opened it to find two sheets of paper. The one yellowed with age I opened first.

"Oh, my gosh," I exclaimed. "That's the map Woodie and I drew over 50 years ago in Boo-ditch when we buried our treasure." The other sheet was relatively new. She had typed a note to me.

Sonja,

If you are reading this, it means that I have passed away. We have some unfinished business that you will have to take care of. I am depending on you as I depended on your strength all those growing up years.

I saved our map hoping that some day we would go back and dig up our treasure. Our lives went in different directions. Even though I never forgot, the time was never right to go back. I hid this map in an envelope under a loose brick in our 'porch' hide-a-way. It kept dry all those years.

When we moved, I hid it inside my jewelry box in the hidden compartment. When mother and dad died, I took it out, put it in another envelope, wrote this note and put them inside my will.

You see, that rhinestone broach I put in the box was really made of diamonds that had belonged to my grandmother. It had fallen off of mother's dress one night onto the rug. The catch was broken. I found it and kept it for our treasure chest. Mother looked and looked for it. Finally she assumed that the maid had taken it.

I never could tell mother that I had taken (or stolen) it especially after we had broken all her plants on the porch using the leaves for money and particularly since we had set fire to the teepee.

Mom and Dad are both gone now. I am not able to go through the thick bamboo to find the place. Maybe you can. If you do succeed, would you please give the pin to my nephew?

Sonja, thank you for your friendship. You made growing up on that lonely road not lonely. You made me forget my handicap with all those wonderful adventures we had.

Love,
Woodie

P. S. I hope you find the treasure. My secret treasure is in that little metal box.

Tears were in my eyes as I handed the letter to Charlie who read it aloud to Will. That was the first time Woodie had ever referred to her handicap.

We all just stared at each other, our mouths gaping, not knowing what to think.

"Well," I said finally. "I'm game, if you are. With a couple of strong guys digging, maybe we can find it."

"I'll go find a shovel," said Charlie. "Will, you want to come with me?"

"Sure," said Will following Charlie. "Gosh this is exciting. Sonja told me about this on the trip down. I had no idea we'd go tromping through the woods...or rather through the bamboo... looking for a lost treasure."

"Me either," said Charlie. "Here are two shovels, Will. You take this one."

We didn't bother to change into "wood tromping" clothes. We just got in the car and headed to the road where Woodie and I once lived. Approaching the road, there was only a humongous hole where my house had been. Someone was getting ready to build condominiums on the site. Then we continued on up the road, now paved, to where Woodie's house had been. It had been sold for $1.00 to someone on the island. They had taken it down and rebuilt it at another location but still on the island.

"Look!" I said. "There are the concrete steps where Woodie and I bounced the balls. Now let me see if I can find where our "porch hide-a-way" was." I said excitedly. I was amazed that there were two foundations where the house had been. One was made of tabby and one of bricks.

"Look!" I said. There are two foundations. That means there was also a house in the same place during plantation days because one of the foundations is made of tabby."

"Now I'm looking for an eleagnus bush." I said.

"A what?" Charlie asked puzzled.

"An elcagnus bush. It was at the corner of the porch where our hide-a-way was."

"Is this it?" asked Will as he pulled off a leaf. "The leaf has rust-colored flecks on it like you described on the way down to the island."

"That's it" I screamed. "I found it! I found it! I can't believe it is still here.

"Me either,! Charlie declared.

"Look at the little berries on it. We used to eat them." I informed. "What are you doing, Will?" I asked as I saw him stooping down.

"Oh, I was just looking to see if you left anything here." he said as he got up.

"Did you find anything" Charlie asked.

"No"

"Well lets continue into the bamboo," Charlie urged.

We all headed toward the nursery. "Let's go in the back way," I said. "I think we can find the ditch quicker."

"Your memory sure is good, Sonja," Charlie said as he pointed to a small indentation (our ditch) in the ground that went into the bamboo.

Ducking down beneath the thick bamboo, we followed the ditch until we came to a rather big oak tree. Well, it was 50 years old.

"That must be the place, Sonja," Charlie said.

"Yeah," said Will. "That must be the oak tree on the map. It's the only oak tree out here."

"Let's see," I said. "We came in from the blue side of the ditch and the treasure was on the red side. Will, your feet are shorter than ours and you are 10 years old. How about walking off the spaces?"

"Sure," said Will ready to start.

"Remember, Sonja," Charlie said. "That oak tree isn't as small as it was then. You'll have to allow for the size of the trunk in counting your steps."

"You are right," I said. "Will, start at the edge of the ditch walking off those paces."

Will started walking in a straight line counting his paces. One, two, three, four, five, six, seven, eight, nine, ten.

"Okay. Now turn to your left and go in a straight line for 10 more steps." I said.

"Is this right?" Will asked, almost losing his balance.

"That's right," said Charlie. "Now turn to the right and go five steps. I'll be there with the shovel to mark the place."

"Here it is, "Will declared. "Let's start digging.

"Let's make a circle about three feet wide around this spot and dig from there." Charlie suggested.

"Good idea," I said. "Maybe we won't miss it. It shouldn't be far under the ground. At least it wasn't 50 years ago."

The boys started digging from the outer side of the circle going down about 8 inches and throwing the dirt off to one side.

It looked like they were digging a moat as they circled around not missing any side. Getting closer to the middle, we all were getting excited, but a little disappointed that we hadn't hit anything. About 10 inches inside on the red side of the circle, Will heard a different sound.

"I've found it. I've found it", he shouted digging faster.

"Hold on a minute, Will," Charlie cautioned. Remember that is an old metal tin and could be very rusty. We don't want to damage it."

"Okay" said Will. "Let me dig away with my hands." Falling on his knees Will scraped away leaves and dirt.

"Here it is. I found it! I found it!" Will exploded. "Help me get this out, Charlie."

They both dug with their hands until all of the top of the box could be seen. Then Charlie pushed the shovel straight down on each side of the box to loosen it from its hole. Finally, he got the shovel under it and pried it up.

"Would you look at that thing?" Charlie said. It's still covered with wax. Let's take it to the house and open it."

Looking in the opposite direction, I remembered the box I had found in the river.

"Hey, Sonja," Will said. "Do you think we could find that other box you buried?

"What's that?" Charlie asked.

"Will, you must have read my thoughts. Oh, Charlie, it's a box I found floating in the river after the two ships were torpedoed off the coast in World War II." I explained.

"Where did you bury it, Sonja?" Charlie asked.

"Just in the opposite direction of this treasure." I said.

"Well, let's count off the paces again,"Charlie said. "No reason to come back out another time. It may never happen."

"That's true, "I confessed. "But remember, this box is bigger and it didn't have wax all over it. But it was water proof because it floated.

Going through the same procedure, we finally found the box, which had dirt all over it but looked sturdy. We hauled it out of the hole and headed back to Woodie's house with two treasure chests.

"Let's open the one you found in the river first," said Charlie.

"I don't have a key. Do you think you could pry it open?" I asked.

Taking out his pocket knife, Charlie worked on the lock. All rusty, it wasn't too hard to open.

Here was history lying in this box. I opened it. Inside was a leather pouch with letters and pictures of a small baby now yellowed with age.

"Oh, my gosh," I said. "This belonged to one of the men on one of the ships. This must have been his child"

"Do you see an address? Maybe a relative is still living at that address." Charlie said.

"Yes, here is one right here." I said. The ink had faded, but I could still make out an address in Michigan. "I am going to find out who this belonged to and return it."

"Hey that's enough of that," Will said. "I want to see what's in your treasure chest."

Charlie scraped all the wax off and pried off the lid. I looked inside and everything looked just like it had on the day we put it in the ground. At least I thought it was, until I lifted the bandana; it was in shreds. All the contents were soon on the table.

There they were: the diamond broach, the bobbie pin–not rusty–the buffalo nickel, the miniature book of St. John, the greenish marble, the string of blue glass beads, the Schaeffer fountain pen, the corsage pin and Woodie's metal lozenge box.

"Well," said Charlie. "You have quite a collection there. You don't find buffalo nickels anymore. And that greenish marble is agate, a shooter. It's quite rare these days."

"Charlie, here's the brooch. Maybe you can get the catch fixed and give it to your wife."

"I'll take the Bible and the metal lozenge box, "I said quickly.

"What's so special about them?" Charlie asked.

"I know! I know!" Will said.

"How can you know?" Charlie was puzzled.

"Sonja, told me. Those are the two things Woodie and Sonja put in the box that neither one knew what the other had put in. They are special treasures that each one had. Sonja's is in the Bible and Woodie's is in the metal box"

"He right, but I want to open these alone." I said rubbing the metal box.

"Will, you take what you want." I continued. "I'm just glad we were able to complete after 60 years, what Woodie I had planned to do a year later back in the 40s."

We cleaned up our mess after making sure that everyone had their treasure.

"Charlie, thanks for calling me and let's keep in touch," I said as Will and I started out the door.

Will and I spent the night on the island in one of the new motels before heading back to Atlanta the next morning. For a while the trip was silent, as Will gazed out the window in deep thought.

I had always teased him with "Will, a penny for your thoughts." This time he answered me.

"Sonja, are you going to let me know what the secret treasures are?"

"Not today, Will. Sometime after I have looked in the box and found what it is...maybe then! Okay?"

"Yeah, its okay. I think I understand, but gosh, Sonja, you and Woodie did so many exciting things. I wish I could have lived back then."

"We did a lot of exciting things, Will," I answered, "but so do you; only in a different way. You go camping with the Boy Scouts, and travel to Cumberland Island in the summer to fish and explore. You just don't spend enough time in any one place to let you imagine all kinds of adventures like we did. But you do have a big back yard."

"Yeah, but there are only swings there," he answered quietly. "I want my own place where I could explore like you did...and with a special friend."

"Well, I can't help you with that, Will. One day you may find your own adventure. But we really had an adventure this weekend, didn't we?"

"It was one I'll never forget, Sonja. I love you."

"And I love you too, Will."

We couldn't know that after hearing about our island adventure, Will's father would build him a "tree house" in their large back yard. Some days Will might make it into a fort; on others it could be a pirate ship flying a home-made Skull and Crossbones on a crooked stick.

One day I would climb the ladder and, peeking in, discover Will's little sterno stove complete with empty sterno can, a few packets of instant grits, a little saucepan with a scorched bottom, an olive jar filled with matches, two spoons, salt, and an unfinished wooden box decorated like a treasure chest; all the ingredients Will would need to recreate an adventure–with some improvements.

But that day in the car, the silence reigned as he again gazed out the window for most of the trip home. I would have given more than a penny for his thoughts but I had my own thoughts and memories to sort.

Epilogue

It took me a year, but I finally located the man whose baby picture I had found in the chest that once floated down the river. He had been 18 months old when his father died at sea. I mailed him the whole box with all the yellowed papers and faded pictures. He was so grateful. Little did I know when I was 10 years old that I was saving some wonderful memories for a son who had never met his father.

I decided not to move back to the island. I've never witnessed another baptism by the river. The waterfront fumed with motorboats, trailers and docks. Concrete slabs form a wall into which sand was pushed into destroying the shoreline. There is no way to walk down the bluff and into the water. There is no bluff. Our home site with the house dad built had to be sold. Unattractive condominiums towered the landscape. Saws destroyed the graceful arms of the ancient live oaks and the nail and stob. One can't live where the aura and beauty and signs of days gone by have been destroyed.

I moved to a small quiet town on the coast creating new memories. I can in this serene setting sit on my porch in my rocking chair in the late afternoon and recapture those childhood memories.

One evening while rocking on my porch, I took out the treasures that Woodie and I had buried. In the middle of the Bible was my treasure written on a scrap of yellowed paper. I unfolded it. I didn't need to read it because I had memorized the words long ago... "Roses are red. Violets are purple. We make a friendship circle." Childish words, but with great truth.

Opening the rusty lozenge box I found folded inside another scrap of yellowed paper. In Woodie's scrawling I read: "Roses are red. Violets are blue. I treasure you most, for your heart is true. Bamboo is green. Spanish Moss is gray. My secret treasure is you, for you help me everyday."

As tears rolled down my cheeks I reflected on the skinny, lame determined child I had played with who couldn't speak clearly or write legibly but her thoughts were beautifully expressed. Memories and friends are treasures for life.

Facts:

Woodie and Sonja were real. I even used their real names. Woodie was a determine girl. She wanted to be normal physically and strived all her life to be so. Once when I was on St. Simons with my sister, Thora, we arranged to have Thora stay with Mrs. Estes while I took Woodie out to dinner. When I went by to get her, she had prepared a sandwich lunch for us all and refused any help in getting ice or pouring tea or cleaning up.

Many, many years ago I had this idea of writing about our childhood. Woodie was all in favor of it and her mother encouraged her as she needed something else to keep her mind occupied. Woodie had learned to use the typewriter and sent me one story. I combined it with a couple of other episodes and sent them all to her hoping that she would contact a local newspaper to put in a series. Of course, that didn't work, so we just left it alone, but the idea was always in the back of my mind to write about growing up with a playmate who had cerebral palsy in an area of St. Simons no one hardly knew about until Eugenia Price wrote her trilogy. I have included the story Woodie sent me and you can tell that we had the same thoughts about our childhood.

I didn't go to some other place to live, but moved home and live in Brunswick, Georgia, just across the causeway from St. Simons Island.

Live Oaks and Treasures
by
Woodie Angela Estes

Those wonderful old oak trees which lined Gascoigne Bluff for hundreds of years were not only gainfully used in building ships, as "Old Ironsides," they were like a powerful drug to two little girls living in their midst.

One particularly bewitching oak tree was located just on the curve going up to my house. It's full branches gracefully fell to just a few feet off the ground, which meant Sonja and I could pull the limbs down far enough to start our climb up through its myriad twists and turns, until our stomachs told us we were high enough. Then as we picked our perches and settled back, hidden in the leaves, we looked out, for what seemed to us, miles of "our land." Hours were spent watching for real and imagined "outsiders" going about their business below us. Our imaginations were so primed that we saw pirates, Indians, you name it, stalking under our watchful eyes. When we tired of this spying one of us would climb down to the ground, catch hold of the biggest limb and PULL. This made the greatest swing we could devise. Taking turns, we gave the other a real ride, which felt as though we were sailing through the tops of the trees. Finally, one would tire or the other call "uncle" then we would both climb down and plot our next escapade. I'm sure our parents often wondered if we would survive without broken necks to adulthood.

Why we were so intrigued by pirates, I don't recall, unless it was living on the Frederica River banks and hearing tales told by Sonja's brother, Bubber, who took great pleasure in tormenting us.

After we made our hide-away "Boo-Ditch," which was in a great stand of bamboo behind my house, where my father and King helped us build our teepee of burlap bags covering several bamboo canes tied together to form a cone effect. One of our first ideas was we must lay claim to this land. What to do? Of course, we just needed to gather a treasure chest of our most prized possessions and bury it! In went "jewels", money (perhaps all of 25 cents each), and one special keepsake—this had to be authentic in order to work—placed them in a container to keep out water or other foreign objects and took it to Boo-Ditch along with a knife, very dull, and a small shovel from our sand pile. We very carefully picked our starting point and marked it, a small tree, with a slash of our trusty, rusty knife, taking exact steps, we thought, we made so many steps forward, found a rock planted it there, so many steps to the left and bent a twig to show our next move, then so many steps to the right, where a small bush had conveniently sprung up, and finally so many steps forward to a completely bare spot, there could be no signs of anything at this strategic point, and plunked down to rest. It got hot in that bamboo patch! Taking a few sips of water from our jug, Sonja started digging a hole large enough to conceal our "treasure." Bamboo is notorious for it's root system, not only is it very touch, there is an absolute mass of cross fibers.

By the time the digging process was completed, we were two tired, but undaunted youngsters. By now the sun was also going down and we knew we would be in big trouble if we didn't get home before our parents missed us.

Hastily we dropped the loot into the hole and covered it back up. Now, of course we KNEW exactly where this spot was. After all, hadn't we carefully filed this information in our heads as we went along, plus all of the "Indian signs" we made?

Why, then, several weeks later, when we retraced our steps and dug, there was nothing but dirt? We repeated this process over and over to no avail. If they ever start digging in that bamboo patch in preparation for condominiums or some such nonsense, maybe our "treasure" will be uncovered. Did we forget something, did the signs change, or what happened to our precious collection? This still remains one of our mysteries 45 years (now it's 70 yrs)later. WHO KNOWS?

✼ ✼ ✼

I must confess that this is a "non-fiction-fiction" story. The characters are true, the situation is true and most of the episodes are true, but not all just as the are depicted. Call that "poetic license"...Sonja Olsen

Caption: LtoR: Sonja and Woodie in Sonja's front yard. Nine Years Old.

✡ ✡ ✡

Made in the USA
Charleston, SC
30 November 2012